PRAISE FOR
GERALD PETIEVICH
AND
THE QUALITY OF THE INFORMANT

"*THE QUALITY OF THE INFORMANT* IS GERALD PE-TIEVICH'S FIFTH FORAY INTO DETECTIVE FICTION, AND ONCE AGAIN HE DELIVERS A HARD-HITTING, GRITTY AND ACTION-FILLED TALE OF THE UNDER-WORLD OF THIEVERY. THE FINALE . . . IS AS EX-PLOSIVE AS IT IS GORY. THE DIALOGUE IS TERSE, STACCATO; THE ATMOSPHERE IS SQUALID, SLEAZY AND HARROWING; AND THE PACE IS UNWAVER-INGLY FAST. . . . PETIEVICH BRINGS A POWERFUL NOTE OF AUTHENTICITY TO THIS STORY."

—*Los Angeles Herald-Examiner*

"GERALD PETIEVICH RETURNS WITH ANOTHER WILD ESCAPADE FEATURING CHARLES CARR, THE EPITOME OF A BRASH U.S. AGENT. PETIEVICH WRITES WITH A SWIFT INTENSITY. . . . THE ONLY QUESTION IS WHETHER CARR OR HIS ADVERSARY WILL SURVIVE."

—*St. Louis Post-Dispatch*

"GERALD PETIEVICH'S BOOKS CRACKLE WITH AUTHENTICITY. . . . THEY ALSO FEATURE GREAT STORIES, CHARACTERS THAT JUMP OFF THE PAGE AT YOU AND CRISP DIALOGUE. IT'S A COMBINA-TION THAT'S IRRESISTIBLE."

—*Grand Rapids Press*

(more)

Books by Gerald Petievich

The Quality of the Informant
Shakedown
To Die in Beverly Hills
To Live and Die in L.A.

Published by POCKET BOOKS

Most Pocket Books are available at special quantity discounts for bulk purchases for sales promotions, premiums or fund raising. Special books or book excerpts can also be created to fit specific needs.

For details write the office of the Vice President of Special Markets, Pocket Books, 1230 Avenue of the Americas, New York, New York 10020.

THE QUALITY
OF THE
INFORMANT

GERALD PETIEVICH

POCKET BOOKS

New York   London   Toronto   Sydney   Tokyo   Singapore

POCKET BOOKS, a division of Simon & Schuster Inc.
1230 Avenue of the Americas, New York, NY 10020

For
JOHN,
GUDRUN,
TRIXI
and
JOHNNY

THE QUALITY OF THE INFORMANT

CHAPTER 1

Though it was early in the day the Castaways Lounge had plenty of customers, mostly men. The walls of the dimly lit bar were decorated with crude glow-in-the-dark paintings of nude women with heavy breasts and luminous pink nipples. There were lots of whispered conversations about money, calls made from the pay phone next to the rest room, sudden departures and returns. There were many bars like it in Hollywood.

Paul LaMonica sat at a cocktail table with Teddy Mora, a gaunt man with an oatmeal complexion. The meeting had been Mora's idea. He said he had a proposition.

"I've just lined up the best coke connection on the West Coast," Mora said. "They call him the Barber. He's a hair stylist who makes house calls to the movie stars; I mean the *big* movie stars. He told me they don't even haggle price. They like cocaine and they don't give a shit what it costs."

"So?" LaMonica said. He sipped a Bloody Mary.

"So, his supplier got himself killed on a rip-off day before yesterday," Mora said. "The Barber wants me to take over. The man needs dope for the movie stars. This is the chance of a lifetime."

"Where do I fit in?" La Monica asked.

"I need front money for the first load of snow," Mora said. "I'm offering you the chance to go in with me. We'd be partners. The way I have it figured, we can triple our investment with every load."

LaMonica lit a cigarette. "Dope is not my thing," he said. "I don't even know enough about it to talk price. Besides, every deal has a thousand middlemen involved, and from what I've seen through the years, one of 'em is usually a snitch." He frowned. "And I don't like snitches."

"I'm not asking you to get involved in any of the negotiations," Teddy Mora said. "I can handle the nitty-gritty. You're an ink-and-paper man and you always have been. I know that." Mora reached across the table and patted the other man on the arm in a brotherly fashion. "All I'm asking you to do is to come in as a partner; to make an investment. You'll come straight in from the top end of the thing. I'll handle all the details. There is virtually no risk whatsoever. I guarantee that."

A ginger-haired cocktail waitress came to the table. Her name tag read "Linda" and she wore a low-cut top and a short skirt. "Another round?" she said. La Monica nodded. As she emptied the ashtray her leg rubbed against his arm. She smiled at him and walked away. He guessed her age as close to forty, a few years younger than his. "How much are we talking about?" LaMonica asked. He rubbed his hands together.

"We need a total of a hundred," Mora said. "My fifty grand is in the bank right now."

"How do I know that?" LaMonica had a wry smile.

Teddy Mora reached into his back pocket, pulled out a bankbook, and handed it to LaMonica. LaMonica opened the book. There were a dozen or so stamped entries totaling about fifty thousand dollars. He handed the book back.

"Okay," LaMonica said. "I come up with fifty . . . then what?" He took a drag from the cigarette and picked a piece of tobacco off the end of his tongue.

"Then we deposit the money into a bank account in Ensenada," Mora said. "An hour later we get a telephone call.

The load will be stashed in a car in the tourists' parking lot on the U.S. side of the border. We pick up the load and head for L.A., where the Barber is waiting. He pays *us* up front and we tell *him* where to find the package. We triple our hundred grand in one day. On our end, it's just you and me. You don't have to meet anyone. There is no way for anything to go wrong. On the Mexican side, the deal is insured by my contacts in Mexico City. When I say 'contacts', I'm talking about people at the highest level. I'm talking about the *politicos*. It's taken me three years of living in Mexico to set this thing up."

LaMonica raised his eyebrows in an expression of disbelief. "Why don't you just parlay two deals for fifty each? Why do you need me?"

"Good question," Mora said. "The answer is that I've been talking a big game to the Barber, but now that the connection has finally come together, I'm short of cash. I've got a lot of money tied up in my bar in Ensenada, and I just bought a head shop down the street from here by Grauman's Chinese. I'm short of bucks. It's that simple. I'm giving you a shot at the deal because I trust you; we walked the yard together. If you'll come in with me I won't have to worry about talking this thing up to investors and taking the chance of meeting a fed or an informer. But I hope you're realistic enough to see that there are plenty of people who would literally *jump* on this thing."

Mora picked up his drink and took sips, then set the glass down. His hands grasped the edge of the table. He leaned forward and said, "What I'm telling you is that you can fuck around for the rest of your life with funny money and phony checks and you will never be able to score anywhere near what you could with just *one* solid coke deal. I don't have to sit here and remind you that bogus bills have to be passed *one at a time,* or at best, dealt off in thousand-dollar packages to a parade of sniffling, back-stabbing hypes, one out of two of which is a rat. Even checks . . . top limit can't be more than a few grand *and* you have to stand there in the bank with your face hanging out in order to cash it." Mora pulled his chair closer to the table. "Coke is the *answer*. There's guys who have made enough to walk away from everything for once and for all. And I'm not talking about heavies. I'm talking about twenty-one-year-old red-assed punks sailing around on their yachts in Marina Del Rey *right this very minute*. They had the guts to get in their car and make one round-trip from here to Tijuana and back. L.A. is full of people like that. And what the hell did they have to lose? Minimum, straight probation for the first offense; or maximum, a year in a federal camp with tennis courts. Was it worth it? You're goddamn fucking *right* it was. Why? Because there's a market for the shit! The movie stars, TV people, doctors, dentists . . . *they pack their noses every night.* They get *off* on it! And, old buddy, most important of all, they are willing to *pay out their asses* for it."

Having spit out the last sentence, Teddy Mora sat back in his chair and folded his arms across his chest.

LaMonica smiled. "I guess after all these years I can trust you not to try to scam me," he said.

Linda the waitress leaned back against her bar station and gazed in his direction. She popped an olive into her mouth and made a funny face. LaMonica smiled.

"I've always made it a point not to cross Paulie LaMonica," Mora said. "It's because I know you too well. Friend or not, you'd kill me and sit down and eat a sandwich afterward." Mora laughed nervously.

The waitress approached them, and they stopped talking. As she arranged drinks on the table she made a point of giving LaMonica an extra peek down the front of her low-cut costume.

LaMonica paid her. "Keep the change."

"Thank you, Silver Fox," she said with a smile.

As she walked away he noticed that her legs were smooth, no varicose veins. All in all, a reasonably attractive woman.

Mora's leering eyes followed the waitress back to the bar. "Word is she can suck a tennis ball through a twenty-foot garden hose," he whispered.

Linda set the empty drinks down on the bar. She turned and winked at LaMonica. He winked back.

"It'll take me a week or two to come up with my fifty grand," LaMonica said. "I have a *thing* mapped out."

"We've got to move on this deal as soon as we can," Mora said. "The buyer won't wait forever. He's *big*, I'm telling ya. He gets invited to every studio party. He's the *dope pusher to the stars*."

CHAPTER 2

The air-conditioning unit in the modest apartment had just clicked off. Its rattle was replaced by the *whiz-hum* sound of the nearby Hollywood freeway.

Linda Gleason was in her bedroom, standing in front of a dressing-table mirror. She reached behind for the zipper, tugged at it, and the cocktail waitress outfit split in half. She gave a shrug and it dropped to the floor.

In her underwear she turned and faced the man sitting on the edge of the bed. She knew him only as Paul, and his hair was styled, graying, perhaps dyed. His pants were off. He had the paunch, the fish-skin folds on the belly, that all the Hollywood rounders, the credit-card bullshitters, the confidence men with open-collar Beverly Hills shirts wore like a uniform. To her, it was a telltale mark of prison.

But there were other signs: his generally cautious demeanor; the vague remarks on the telephone; his reluctance to leave messages or to tell her where he lived; the way he parked his car around the corner from the Castaways Lounge rather than in the parking lot. And the missing little finger . . . could he have lost it in a prison knife fight?

The only thing she liked about the man so far was the way he had come right out and put the question to her. No beating-around-the-bush crap about "going out for break-fast" or "taking a drive to the beach." His had been a simple and straightforward "Let's fuck." (Much to his surprise, she'd said, "Shouldn't we wait until we get to my apartment?") Even as a teenager she had preferred the boys who straight-out pulled her sweater off over those who insisted on the crawling-hands-breath-holding-kissy-face act before getting down to business. Of course she had learned early on that women could not express such thoughts. Richard, her dead husband, had made that point more than once. "It kills the mystery," he'd said.

"Small world," Linda said, unsnapping her bra.

"Like how?" Paul pulled off his undershirt and tossed it on the floor. He had a florist's smile.

"You having known my husband," she said, shrugging off the bra and sitting down at the dressing table. As she ran a brush through her hair she watched him in the mirror. He leaned back against the headboard.

"Richard and I were at Terminal Island together ten years ago," he said. "Maximum security. I heard about what happened to him after we got out. Too bad." He said "too bad" without shaking his head. He pulled off his shorts and tossed them on the floor.

Linda leaned close to the mirror and applied lipstick. "I told him it would happen if he took money from a loan shark, but he never listened to me . . . or to anyone else, for that matter." She made her lips flat and pressed them together.

The man's hand was between his legs. He was pulling on himself. Linda hoped it wouldn't mean one of those marathon efforts to make him come. At least he wasn't drunk, she thought.

Linda Gleason stood up and pulled off her panties. She tossed them at a chair. Crawling onto the bed, she perched on her knees in front of him. "Relax," she said. "Let me do everything." Without hesitation, she took his cock firmly in her hand and pumped gently. "Tell me what you like," she whispered.

The man gave a moan and soon became erect. He whispered things for her to do, positions to assume, and she complied. None of the requests surprised her. It was the usual bill-of-fare fantasy cock-worship act that always excited men. Hurrying like an adolescent, he was on top of her, rutting, sweating, exercising his ugly abdomen, and Linda made periodic joy-yelps to help him along. Finally, his eyes closed and he gave in to orgasm. As the man groaned in a wave of pleasure, Linda glanced at a clock on the nightstand. She made an expected *aaaah* sound. With a wet kiss, he rolled off her in exhaustion.

Linda snuggled next to him. Her hand danced gently across the hair on his chest for a while. "Mmmm," she said. "It's nice to be with someone who turns me on."

Paul fondled a breast. "I don't come to L.A. very often," he said. "The feds here are looking for me."

Linda's neck tingled. She had guessed right. "Why?" she asked.

"Funny money." He flicked her nipple.

Hiding her excitement at the remark, Linda took his hand and covered it with little kisses. "When are you leaving town?"

"Tomorrow night," Paul said, looking at the ceiling.

During the next half hour or so, they showered separately and Paul dressed.

While Linda stood drying off in front of the bathroom door, Paul said something about using the telephone. Tucking in his shirt, he went into the living room.

Linda tiptoed to the half-closed door as he was dialing the phone.

"This is Robert French," she heard him say. "May I speak to Mr. Lassiter please?"

Linda put her ear to the crack of the door.

"Hello, Robert French here," Paul said. "I ordered thirty reams of safety paper and some inks yesterday. Would you check and see if the order is ready?" Nothing was said for a while. Then, "Fine," Paul said. "No, that won't be necessary. I'll be in to pick it up. Thanks." He hung up the phone and made another call. "Yes, for one month only," he said. "I want you to answer: 'International Investigations Incorporated.' I'll call in for messages once a day. Whoever calls, just tell them I'm out of town." He hung up the receiver.

Linda dashed to the closet and grabbed a robe. Paul came back into the bedroom and sat down on the bed. He started putting on his shoes.

"Sounds like you've got something cooking," Linda said, fearing to be any more direct. She ran a brush through her damp hair.

"You might say that," Paul said. "Matter of fact, I'll be needing a female backup in a week or so. Interested?"

Linda shrugged and continued to brush. She wished she'd had a chance to look through his wallet. "Tomorrow is my day off," she said, sitting down next to him on the bed. "How about coming over before you leave. We can barbecue steaks." She nuzzled his ear. "And maybe I can have a repeat performance before I let you go," she whispered, giving his crotch a squeeze.

"Why not," he said proudly. He stood up and threw on his camel's-hair sport coat. Linda followed him to the front door.

He patted her on the bottom and said, "See ya tomorrow," in a confident tone. Linda Gleason winked. The man walked outside.

Having closed and bolted the door, she found her purse on the kitchen counter, dug out a pack of filter tips and lit up. Plopping down on the sofa, she grabbed the phone off the coffee table and dialed.

A sleepy-voiced man answered. "U.S. Treasury Field Enforcement."

"I'm trying to get in touch with Special Agent Charles Carr," Linda Gleason said. She took a deep drag on the cigarette and blew out a stream of smoke.

"He works the four-to-twelve shift. Would you like to leave a message?"

"I'll call later, thanks."

The phone clicked.

• • •

It was 3:00 P.M.

The apartment's solitary bedroom was bare except for a bed with a suitcase opened on it and a dresser. The second-story view from the window was of another apartment house. In Santa Monica, a blocked ocean view was the sign of an affordable address.

Having shaved, showered, and donned slacks and a short-sleeved white shirt with a frayed collar, Charles Carr fastened a holster to his belt. He realized as he dressed that he had taken the shirt with him to Washington, D.C., when he'd been transferred there from L.A. two years ago. Unable to find his handcuff case after rummaging through the suitcase, he hung the cuffs over his belt at the small of his back. He shoved his .38 into the holster.

While shaving, he had momentarily considered leaving the stubble on his upper lip to begin a mustache. A lady bartender he'd dated in D.C. had once told him it would make him look younger. He had quickly scotched the daydream and shaved clean. So he looked like a fifty-year-old man with a barroom flush on his cheekbones—so what? The Treasury Department's requirements had been for veterans with 20/20 vision and "no distinguishing traits." Though his looks, dress, and general demeanor might keep him from making it to the pages of *Gentleman's Quarterly,* he figured he still filled the bill as a street-level T-man.

He emptied his suitcase of the personal items he always seemed to cart along with him from transfer to transfer: a grainy Treasury Agent Training School class photo with everyone wearing hats; old bullet pouches and scribbly address books; a printed invitation to a 101st Airborne reunion decorated with a map of Korea; a news clipping about his shoot-out with the hired killer Clyde Reno; a dog-eared photograph of his mother and father sitting on the front porch of their tiny home in Boyle Heights; a stack of letters from Sally Malone. He stuffed the items into dresser drawers.

Because his belongs were being shipped by government bill of lading (known to federal civil servants as the Wagon Train), he had no utensils. At the kitchen sink, he rinsed out a Styrofoam cup he found in the cabinet and drank two cups of water. He left the apartment and headed downtown.

A tepid Santa Ana wind swirled in the open windows of Charles Carr's sedan as he sped east along the Santa Monica freeway. The breeze had wafted the city's stultifying layer of smog to sea, revealing a panorama of chaparral-covered foothills and mountains extending from Hollywood east past Cucamonga: nature's infrequent reminder that without neon, asphalt, Chevron stations, and tract homes with television aerials, Los Angeles was a desert basin touching an ocean.

Years ago he had chased a counterfeiter at more than a hundred miles an hour along the same freeway. Each of the familiar exit signs stirred other such memories; a rooftop chase along LaCienega; a three-week surveillance on Sepulveda; a shoot-out in front of a bank on Robertson Boulevard. Hell, he had chased paper pushers and passers around the city for so long that few streets were unfamiliar to him. It was no secret that he thrived on the big-city action: the bizarre people, the jungle politics of the underworld, the challenge of trying to beat the counterfeiters and hoods at their own game.

Off duty, his activities centered around police watering holes, maudlin retirement-and-promotion parties, barroom celebrations after big cases, and Dodger games. Though his attachments to women were usually characterized by casual dates and one-night stands, this was due to no particular creed or philosophy.

Certainly by any normal standards his existence could be described as neither wholesome nor particularly fruitful. But for a man who more than twenty years ago had *volunteered* for the army—the 101st Airborne, and combat in Korea—it was not without its rewards.

At Vermont Avenue he pulled into the slow lane and took the turnoff. He headed north through a crowded business district. At the edge of Hollywood, he pulled up in front of a fast-food stand, a four-seater operation fashioned out of sheet metal that had been painted bright red. On the awning over the stools was a crudely painted sign of a hot dog dripping with mustard: "Calhoun's" was lettered on the bun. Charles Carr parked his sedan and got out.

"The Snake has returned," Calhoun said as Carr straddled a stool. The 260-pound black man wore a white T-shirt and trousers, apron, and a paper chef's hat. Without using tongs, he plopped a frankfurter into a bun. Having loaded the bun with relish and mustard, he wrapped the hot dog and set it down in front of Carr. Calhoun wiped his fingers on a rag. The men shook hands, "Kelly told me you'd transferred back," Calhoun said. "I've been waiting for you to stop by."

Carr picked up the hot dog and took a bite. He chewed and swallowed. "What's going on?" he said.

"There's some twenties and phony driver's licenses around," Calhoun said. "Nothing really hot and heavy, you understand. Just the usual. If you want it, it's out there."

"Money talks," Carr said casually. He took another bite.

"You got that right," Calhoun said. "Just wave a little of that green shit around a few people, and a man can get *exactly* what he wants. Hell, yesterday the dude who lives next door told me he could get any brand of TV I wanted. It'll be stolen, but I could actually order the brand I wanted ahead of time. Can you believe that shit?"

Carr nodded. He finished the hot dog.

Calhoun plopped another frankfurter into a bun. Carr gestured no, and Calhoun tossed the frank back in the steamer.

"How's your son doing?" Carr asked.

Calhoun shook his head. "Tyrone's gotten worse since I wrote you that letter," he said. "He won't listen to me and he calls his mother names. It's all because he moved into an apartment with a bunch of jive-ass niggers. A couple of weeks ago I drove him down to the army recruiting office. A sergeant gave him a real nice talking-to. He actually got him to fill out all the papers and take a physical. He was ready to go. The wife and I were all set to have a real nice going-away party for him—a barbecue in Griffith Park." Calhoun adjusted his cap and shook his head again. "Then

22

those jive-ass punks he's been hanging around with talked him out of it. They told him he was an asshole for wanting to go in the army and be a paratrooper. They're dope dealers, a bunch of jack-jawed no-good hophead mother-fuckers. I know they're into funny money too. I heard my boy whispering on the telephone about it. At first I figured I'd go over there and cave their damn heads in, but I'd be taking a chance at ending up in San Quentin my own self. I'm afraid that once I got started I wouldn't know when to quit. You know how I am."

Carr nodded.

A gray-faced old man wearing a filthy baseball cap and T-shirt sat down at the counter. Calhoun served him a hot dog and a cup of coffee. He returned to Carr. "Them jive-ass punks my boy is living with all drive *Cadillacs*. I raised my son in the Baptist Church. I saw to it that his ass was in Sunday school all the way through the tenth grade. But now he's eighteen years old and he's met some punks that deal dope and have enough money to drive their bitches around in *Cadillacs*." He slapped the counter violently. "Damn! And to think my boy came within an inch of being an airborne trooper. He woulda been a second-generation paratrooper instead of a goddamn hophead."

"A person can't even eat a hot dog in peace," said the old man at the counter. He stood up angrily and walked away with his frankfurter and coffee.

Calhoun tipped his hat at the man.

"On second thought, maybe I will have another," Carr said.

Calhoun winked. He prepared a hot dog and handed it to Carr. "Tyrone just don't *know* any better. He's grown up in the city and it's all he knows. He's at the age where he needs a change in environment . . . to find out that there's other people in the world besides the punks that live around the corner. I was the same way when I was his age. I know what I'm talking about."

"The boy needs to jump out of an airplane," Carr said.

Calhoun folded his arms and leaned forward over the

counter. "Or have the jumpmaster kick his ass out the door," he said.

Carr took a bite of the hot dog. He wiped his mouth with a paper napkin. "Still wearing 'em?" he said.

Calhoun stepped back from the counter and held up his foot. The black, round-toed paratrooper's boot had an even shine. "I've had 'em resoled more than thirteen times," he said.

"I'll need an address," Carr said.

Calhoun smiled. He dug a pencil out of a drawer and scribbled something on a napkin. He handed it to Carr.

Carr stuffed the napkin into his wallet. He finished the hot dog, stood up to leave, and said, "Be home tonight."

"I'll be standing by, Sarge," Calhoun said.

CHAPTER 3

The squad-room walls were covered with federal wanted posters, blowups of counterfeit twenties, and street maps dotted with red stickpins.

Charles Carr swiveled his desk chair around to look out the window. The view below was of downtown Los Angeles in darkness: lifeless buildings, grayish-white streetlights, and a freeway still bustling even after rush hour. Across the road the neon lamps of Chinatown gave off an exotic rainbow glimmer. He was glad to be back.

He thumbed through the latest stack of L.A. area intelligence reports, squinting as he turned the pages. He would not give in to wearing glasses.

Jack Kelly, a man of Carr's age with the jaw and limbs of a grizzly bear, hunched at the desk next to him. Tacked to the bulletin board behind his desk was a watercolor of an automobile that looked like a box with wheels. "To Daddy from Junior" was printed in a child's letters along the bottom. "Did you find yourself an apartment?" he asked without looking up.

"Santa Monica," Carr said. "Same building I lived in before I was transferred." He shook his head. "Rent's up a hundred bucks."

Kelly put down the newspaper. "Doesn't seem like two years," he said, chuckling harshly. "The memos 'No Waves' sent to headquarters to keep you from transferring back here were classic. He'd say things like, 'Agent Carr would benefit, *career-wise*, by a transfer to an office other than Los Angeles,' or 'Office requirements in the Senior Special Agent category are minimal . . .' Like the pencil-neck geek that he is, he would never just come out like a man and say he hated your guts and didn't want you here. Good old true-to-form Norbert C. Waeves, the man who can grind out government memos faster than an offset printing press."

Carr smiled and said, "That's why he was promoted to special agent in charge."

Kelly changed the subject. "I saw Sally in court the other day. She wants you to call her . . . told me that three times. Said she had been elected president of the Federal Court Stenographers Association. Nice gal, Sally, lots of class. The wife still says you should have married her years ago."

Carr shrugged.

Kelly folded the newspaper and tossed it in the trash can. "Since you were transferred, here's what you've missed: We have a new United States attorney. He was appointed because he's married to the daughter of that guy that owns half the hotels in Palm Springs. He has Jell-O for brains and all of his prosecutors are family friends—arrogant hippies and unbelievable Ivy League pricks. They're more concerned with the rights of the defendant than the public defender, and they all wear bow ties like that store-front lawyer on television. The other day the U.S. attorney actually gave a press release on the prosecution of a post-man who got caught throwing his advertising mail in the sewer. The same day I asked them for a search warrant for a counterfeiter's car. They refused to issue one because they weren't sure of the case law. I had to let the guy drive off even though I knew the car had a load of phony twenties in the trunk."

"In other words, the system hasn't changed," Carr said.

"What system?" Kelly said. He flipped open a briefcase that was sitting on his desk and grabbed a sandwich. He removed the wax paper and lifted the top piece of bread to check the contents, then mashed the sandwich down with the heel of his hand.

"Meatloaf and raw onions?" Carr said.

Kelly's eyes said yes. He opened his mouth as wide as possible, bit off a full third of the sandwich, and chewed intently. Three more bites and the sandwich disappeared. He pulled a handkerchief from his back pocket and wiped his hands and mouth roughly.

Later, they left the office with Carr behind the wheel of the government sedan. Carr explained Calhoun's problem as they drove south on Main Street past L.A.'s skid row.

"Now I see why you didn't want to talk in the office," Kelly said when Carr finished explaining his plan. He stared at a group of derelicts huddled under a rescue-mission sign featuring a picture of Jesus with outstretched hands. They were passing around a bottle of wine.

"Every one of 'em has a full head of hair," Kelly said.

"Howzat?"

"Winos," Kelly said. "They all have full heads of hair."

Carr gave his old partner a puzzled look.

"Just think of it," Kelly said. "In your whole entire lifetime, how many bald winos have you seen? There must be something about the booze that helps 'em keep their hair."

"Dr. Jack Kelly," Carr said. He chuckled.

Carr steered through the deserted garment district and down Central Avenue past crowded soul-food stands and pool halls. "There's still not one single movie theater in all of Watts," Kelly said. "Too much vandalism, too many fights. But there *is* an answer. The owner could hook electrical wires under every seat in the theater. Anybody causes trouble, just give 'em a jolt. Knock 'em right out the door."

"Great idea," Carr said dryly. He pulled out the napkin to check the address, then turned onto a side street. He parked in front of a run-down apartment house with three Cadillacs lined up in the driveway. The agents took flashlights from the glove compartment and climbed out of the sedan. They strolled slowly down the driveway. Kelly flashed a beam of light on a mailbox. The name *Calhoun* was listed on the box for apartment number 3 along with two other names. Kelly flashed the light on the side of the two-story building. Number 3 was on the ground floor.

"I'll take the back," Kelly whispered. He tiptoed along the driveway and turned right at the corner of the building.

As Carr approached the front door, he heard the sound of rock music inside. He knocked. Footsteps came to the door and a man inside said, "Who's there?" Carr slipped his revolver out of its holster.

"Federal officers," Carr said. "Open the door." There was the sound of running inside. Carr stepped back, lifted his foot, and slammed it into the doorknob as hard as he could. The doorjamb shattered and the door flew open. The living room was empty. He ran down the hallway and into a bedroom. The window was open and a black man was halfway out. He moaned. Kelly had him in a headlock. Carr grabbed the black man by the belt, pulled him back into the room, then threw him against a wall and frisked him. Carr handcuffed the man's hands behind his back. As Kelly started to climb in the window, Carr silently pointed at the closet.

"What's your name?" Carr said to the prisoner.

"Tyrone Calhoun," he said in a voice that quavered.

Carr stepped to the closet door. He stood to the side, grasped the doorknob, and yanked the closet open. Two young black men stood huddled in the corner. "Good evening, lads. Come on out and join the party," he said. The men stepped out of the closet. They wore bright full-sleeved silk shirts and tailored trousers. Carr shoved them against a wall. He frisked them.

As Kelly crawled in the window, Carr motioned him to watch Calhoun. He grabbed the other two men, shoved them into the living room, and opened the front door. "'Bye," he said. The men looked at one another, then rushed out the door and down the driveway. Carr returned to the bedroom.

Kelly pulled drawers out of the dresser and upended them. He yanked clothing out of the closet, searched it, and tossed it on the floor.

"Do you have a warrant?" Tyrone Calhoun said.

"Shut your goddamn mouth," Carr snapped.

Kelly hoisted a nightstand upside down. "Bingo," he said. He tossed Carr a stack of counterfeit ten-dollar bills wrapped with a rubber band.

Carr held the money in front of Calhoun's face. "Is this yours?"

"I just moved in here a couple of weeks ago," Calhoun said. "I swear to God I ain't had anything to do with that stuff."

"Oh, really," Carr said sarcastically. "You're under arrest for possession of counterfeit money." He turned to Kelly. "Give him his rights, Jack."

Kelly sauntered across the room. He pulled a card from his shirt pocket and read in a singsong fashion: "You have the right to remain silent. Anything you say can be used against you in a court or other proceedings. If you cannot afford a shyster one will be appointed for you. You also have a right to a free press and to peaceably assemble for the purpose of libation. Do you understand those rights and wave them as you would the flag of our nation?"

"Uh, yes, sir," Tyrone Calhoun said.

"How old are you?" Carr said.

"I just turned eighteen."

"Then you also have the right to make one telephone call," Carr said. "Whom do you choose to call?"

Tyrone Calhoun squeezed his eyes shut. "My dad will kill me," he said.

Carr grasped the prisoner's arm. He pulled him into the living room. Calhoun gave him a number and Carr dialed it. He held the phone to the young man's ear.

"Dad? It's me. I . . . I'm under arrest, but I didn't do anything. I'm at the apartment."

Carr pulled the phone away and hung up. "I don't like long phone calls," he said.

Kelly shuffled out of the bedroom carrying a handful of pill bottles and glassine envelopes. "Found some dope, too," he said. "The stuff ought to be good for at least another five years in the pen for this punk." He sat down at the kitchen table and made a list of the contraband.

"Where are my, uh, friends?" Tyrone Calhoun asked.

"On their way to jail," Carr said.

A few minutes later, Calhoun, wearing his white uniform, stepped in the door.

"Who are you?" Carr said.

"I'm the boy's father."

"It's not my stuff, Dad," said Tyrone.

"I guess it don't really matter now, do it, *Mr. Jive-Ass?*" Calhoun said.

"The bail will be twenty thousand dollars," Carr said. "We're booking him in at the Terminal Island federal lockup."

"I'm sorry, Dad." His voice cracked.

Calhoun took off his hat. "Officers," he said, "this boy is set to join the U.S. Army. He wants to be a paratrooper. He's done passed the test and filled out all the paperwork. Isn't that right, son?"

The young man gave his father a confused look, then nodded. "I'm supposed to be sworn in any day."

Calhoun straddled a chair at the table. "Officers," he said, "this arrest will ruin the boy's life. It'll mean that he won't get accepted into the army." He hung his head. "If you could see your way to giving the boy a break on this case, I give you my word that he'll go in the army and never cause any trouble again. I'm a member of the Los Angeles Junior Chamber of Commerce."

Kelly continued to write on a pad. "Bullshit," he said.

"I swear he'll take the oath the very moment the recruiting office opens up tomorrow morning," Calhoun said. "Please don't ruin this boy's life."

Carr avoided looking Calhoun in the eye for fear of

laughing. Instead he glared at the young Calhoun with a look of mock enmity for a moment. Then he stood up and nodded at Kelly, who followed him to the corner of the room. They feigned whispering. "You're the boss," Kelly finally said in a louder, disgusted tone. "But I still don't like it." He huffed back to the kitchen table. Angrily, he shoved the counterfeit money and the narcotics into a paper bag and strode out the door.

'I've decided to give the kid a break," Carr said. "But we're keeping the evidence. If he's not sworn into the army and on a bus to basic training by tomorrow night, we'll be out looking for him. I'm holding you personally responsible for what happens."

"You have my word of honor, Officer," the elder Calhoun said. He stood up and shook hands. Carr stepped behind Calhoun and removed his handcuffs.

The young man rubbed his wrists. "Thanks a lot, Officer," he said. "Thanks a lot."

Carr walked out the door. He and Kelly made it into the sedan and closed both doors before they broke into hysterical laughter. Carr caught his breath. "Operation Shanghai."

Kelly kept laughing. He used the back of his hand to wipe away tears of mirth. "After his first day of basic training, he'll wish he'd gone to jail instead!" The laughter continued all the way back to the Federal Building. Before entering the underground garage, Kelly tore up the counterfeit tens and tossed them and the narcotics into a storm drain.

Back in the field office, the phone on Carr's desk rang. He picked up the receiver.

"I heard you were back," Linda Gleason said.

"Long time no see," Carr said.

"I have a homecoming present for you, Charlie."

"And what might that be?"

"A fugitive. Do we have to talk on the phone?"

"I'll come over," Carr said. He hung up and turned to Kelly. "Linda Gleason," he said; "she's got something."

"One good case coming up," Kelly said. "Good ol' Linda is money in the bank."

Carr stood up and put on his suit jacket.

"That's the way it always is," Kelly said. "Good informant, good case; bad informant, bad case. Everything depends on the quality of the informant." Having said this, he picked up the newspaper.

"You're right," Carr said on his way out the door.

CHAPTER 4

As Carr maneuvered the G-car into a hypnotic stream of headlights that was the Hollywood freeway, he pictured Linda five years ago: She was standing in the living room of her apartment; glass was everywhere, the front window blown out by shotgun pellets. She was wearing a housecoat. Her flashing green eyes were minus the map of lines that had developed around them in the years after.

"I knew this would happen eventually," she'd said. "Snitches always get killed." She broke into tears. "I'm gonna get killed just like my husband did."

Carr had put his arm around her shoulder and said, "I'll help you find another place to live. They won't be able to find you again."

He'd helped her pack and put her in a hotel room for the night. A day or so later, he and Kelly moved her into a new apartment and gave her a new name. It was months before Carr succeeded in building up her confidence again. He took her to lunch, sent cards, gave her little tasks; but if there had been any one reason why she'd begun feeding him information about passers and forgers, con men and scam artists again, he would have to say it was the money —Uncle Sam's reward at the end of every case. There was more money for printers and fugitives than phony-twenties passers; but all in all, it was a nice extra income for nothing more than listening to bar talk, getting samples of the current variety of phony paper, making an introduction or two. In this way, she was like most other informants.

A green freeway sign: HOLLYWOOD—NEXT THREE EXITS. Carr swung onto an off ramp that led down a hill. He snaked off the main drag into a residential neighborhood made up of apartment houses that, like everything else in Hollywood, were not worth the money. He parked his car half a block away and walked.

On his way up the street he checked the parked cars. They were all unoccupied. He looked around once more and jogged a few steps into a courtyard with a swimming pool. Linda's apartment was on the first floor. He knocked and she let him in.

Carr made small talk as Linda Gleason, wearing a long dress and a slit up the side, served coffee from a little silver pot. Without asking, she mixed Carr's double cream. It was the ritual of their meetings. She lit a cigarette and sat in a chair across from him.

Linda crossed her legs, making no attempt to cover her thigh. "I don't know Paul's last name," she said. "But he told me he's wanted. He was talking to Teddy Mora for a long time down at the Castaways . . . definitely *business*. Teddy sells any kind of paper he can get his hands on. He only comes in on Fridays; I think he lives out of town. He stays all day and deals paper just to people he knows. He and Paul were talking big figures. Teddy calls him Paulie. I made it a point to meet him because my sixth sense just told me he was a crook. I even had him over here to the apartment and he still wouldn't crack with a last name, though he did tell me he was wanted by the feds for a funny-money caper. I think he's got something cooking right now. He made a couple of phone calls that sounded real strange."

"What kind of calls?" Carr said. He sipped coffee.

"The first call was something about inks and paper," Linda said. "He used the name *Robert French*. The other one might have been to an answering service. He told them to answer the phone by saying, 'International Investigations.'" She puffed her cigarette. "God only knows what kind of scam *that* is."

Carr put his coffee cup down on the table and pulled a pen and notepad out of his coat pocket. "What does he look like?" he said.

"Over forty, medium build, graying hair that might come from a bottle. He has a missing finger—little one, left hand."

Carr made some notes, then put the pen and pad away.

"I've set it up so he'll be coming over here tomorrow afternoon. You can arrest him when he drives up," Linda said.

Carr stood up and sauntered to the door. "I'll check the fugitive files."

Linda was looking at her hands. "If you arrest him, can I get my reward the same day? I've got a few bills to take care of."

"That should be no problem," Carr said.

Carr yanked open a file drawer labeled "Fugitive." He pulled out a stack of brown manila envelopes and spread them out on his desk. It took him an hour to determine that three out of seventy-odd files related to males with the first name Paul. Only one, Paul LaMonica, fit the general description. Carr's finger traced the fine print of the section marked "Physical Characteristics." The amputation was described as "LFT/little/missing." The last line of the run-down sheet read: "Check NCIC for warrant validity." Carr folded the file and slid his chair to the teletype machine a few feet behind him. He typed in LaMonica's name, date of birth, and social-security number, copying the information from the file. He pressed the "end of message" button and waited.

Minutes later, the machine rattled to life again. It typed:

WARRANT VALID/SUBJECT IS FED PRISON ESCAPEE
TERMINAL ISLAND/ARMED & DANGEROUS/U.S. MAR-
SHAL L.A. HOLDS WARRANT. END OF MESSAGE.

The machine stopped. Carr leaned back in his chair and
read the rest of the file carefully. It included a "Synopsis of
Investigation," which read as follows:

LaMonica was the principal in a scheme to cause the
distribution of extremely high-quality counterfeit
hundred-dollar bills. He was able to transact a number
of large purchases of diamonds from legitimate jewelers with the bogus notes. He resold the diamonds to
other jewelers. LaMonica worked alone in the confidence operation and is believed to have printed the
counterfeit notes himself. During the course of the
scheme the subject used various forms of well-made
counterfeit identification. LaMonica has contacts in
Mexico and is believed to be in hiding there.

There was a mug shot photograph of LaMonica stapled
to the inside of the file. Carr ripped the photo off and put it
in his pocket.

It was almost 5:00 P.M.

The atmosphere in Linda's apartment was uneasy. Carr
had been there since noon. Linda was sitting on the sofa,
thumbing through a fashion magazine. They had run out of
small talk. Carr paced in front of the windows. Outside, in
a courtyard decorated with dying Oriental trees in planter
boxes, an old woman with brown spots on her back floated
around a swimming pool on an inflated rubber mattress.
There was no other activity. The mold-colored apartment
doors surrounding the swimming pool might as well have
been nailed shut. Through the wrought-iron fence enclos-
ing the entrance to the complex Carr could see Jack Kelly
leaning back in the driver's seat of the G-car.

Linda picked up the mug shot that was on the coffee
table. It was next to a walkie-talkie radio stenciled PROP-

ERTY OF U.S. GOVT. "His hair is grayer than in that picture," she said. "I think he dyes it."

"It would have been better if you had set up a meeting somewhere other than your apartment," Carr said. He was still looking out the window.

"No matter where or how you arrest him, no matter what time of day or how you do it, in the long run he's going to figure out that I did him," she said.

Carr turned to face the woman. "After we arrest him we can say that we followed him from—"

"It doesn't matter what bullshit story you give him," Linda interrupted. "He'll figure out that I was the snitch. He's not dumb. I'm not worried as long as he goes back to prison. I'm moving to another apartment next week anyway." She ran her hands through her hair, took a deep breath, and exhaled. "How about some coffee?" she said.

"No thanks."

She picked up the walkie-talkie radio and pressed the "transmit" button. "Cup of coffee, Jack?"

"No thanks," Kelly said.

Linda put the radio down. "I hate all the people where I work," she said. "There's no one that's normal. Even the bartenders are ex-cons. Deals go down in there every minute of the day: dope, funny money, hot jewelry, you name it. I don't know how I find these kind of places; come to think of it, they seem to find *me*. Everyone trusts me because I was married to Richard. They think I'm solid." She laughed without smiling.

Nothing was said for a while. Linda flitted about the apartment picking things up, emptying ashtrays. She wiped off the kitchen sink with a sponge. Drying her hands, she turned to Carr. "May I ask you something?" Her tone was soft.

"Shoot," he said.

"After all these years, why haven't you ever made a pass at me? Other men find me attractive . . ." Her smile was wry.

Carr fidgeted. "I guess it's because I don't like to mix business with pleasure," he said.

"Other cops do." She turned to the sink again and filled a coffeepot with water. "You're right," she said. "It would never work. I wouldn't trust you afterward. It's the way I feel about most men who—"

"I think it's him," Kelly blared over the radio. "He's parking across the street . . . getting out of his car."

Carr snapped the blinds closed. He grabbed the radio off the coffee table and pressed the transmit button. "Roger," he said. He leaned close to the blinds and peeked out.

"This is the part I can do without," Linda said. She put the coffeepot down and hurried into the bedroom.

"He's comin' atcha," Kelly announced. "I'll be behind him."

Carr pulled his revolver out of its holster without taking his eyes off the space in the blinds.

The gray-haired man opened the wrought-iron gate and stopped. He looked around for a moment, then strolled to the apartment door and knocked. Carr swung open the door and pointed his revolver at the man's face. "Federal officers, LaMonica. You're under arrest." LaMonica raised his hands. Kelly approached at a full run. He snapped handcuffs on the man's hands.

Linda Gleason came out of the bedroom, a sheepish look on her face. Paul LaMonica stared at her the way inmates stare at prison guards: enmity without expression.

Carr sat in the backseat with LaMonica on the way to the Field Office for the usual processing.

LaMonica was slouched down in the seat. "I wanna do a deal," he said.

Carr was looking out the window at nothing in particular. He didn't answer.

"I know what you're thinking," LaMonica said. "You know my record. I've never cooperated in the past, so why should I now?" He squirmed.

Carr nodded.

"It's because I have enemies at Terminal Island this time. If you send me back there it's the death sentence. I'll get shanked in a week. One of the prison gangs has a contract out on me." LaMonica's eyes were wide. "That's why I had to escape. It was a matter of survival."

Carr reached across the front seat and pulled a booking form from above the visor. He took a pen out of his pocket and filled in LaMonica's name.

LaMonica stared at the form. "I have something to offer, but once you book me it will be too late. Can't we just pull over and chat for a few seconds?"

Carr wrote "Camel's-hair sport coat, brown pants" under a column marked "Prisoner's Clothing." "Mr. LaMonica wants to *chat*," Carr said without looking up.

Kelly laughed.

"I've got a hundred grand in twenties stashed here in L.A.," LaMonica said.

Kelly stopped laughing. His eyes met Carr's rearview mirror. Carr nodded. Kelly steered off the freeway and into a supermarket parking lot. He stopped the car and turned off the engine.

"Where's the stash?" Carr said.

"It's less than ten minutes from here," LaMonica said. "I'm willing to surrender it only in exchange for your promise to let me do my time somewhere other than Terminal Island. Leavenworth, McNeil Island, I don't care. I just can't go back to T.I."

Carr folded the booking card and stuffed it in his coat pocket. "I can't guarantee—"

"I know the program," the prisoner interrupted. "You can't guarantee anything, blah, blah, blah. I also know that for you feds, a prison transfer is no big deal. All I'm asking is that you go to bat for me."

Across the street a Cadillac pulled up to a black woman sitting on a bench at a bus stop. She was wearing a blond wig. The driver of the Cadillac spoke to her through the passenger window. The woman looked around furtively and got in. The car drove off. Shaking his head in disgust, Kelly muttered, "Right in broad daylight."

Carr lit a cigarette and tossed the match out the window. "So you saved some paper for insurance in case you got caught."

"Whatever," LaMonica said with a look of resignation.

"If you lead us to the stash I'll do what I can to keep you out of Terminal Island," Carr said. "That's the only deal I'll go for. No more, no less."

LaMonica leaned his head back against the seat and exhaled. "Okay," he said. "You've got a deal."

"Where to?" said Kelly.

"Head down Hollywood Boulevard," LaMonica said. "It's in a bank safety-deposit box."

Carr dragged on the cigarette. "The key?"

"My wallet," LaMonica said. He leaned toward the window. Carr pulled a wallet from the prisoner's rear pocket. Inside it was a brass key.

"Okay, Jack, now we head for Hollywood," Carr said. Kelly started the engine and got back on the freeway.

LaMonica gave directions to the bank with panache. *"Right turn here, please . . . Left turn here, please."* With manacled hands he pointed to a restaurant with a neon lobster on the roof. "Best lobster in L.A.," he said. "With a little luck I'll be back in there cracking shells in a year or two. Do you figure I'll get much more than that?"

"Depends on the judge," Carr said.

Kelly guffawed. "If you get some pussy like Judge Malcolm he'll probably let you go and put us in jail," he said.

LaMonica pointed out the window. "There's the bank."

Kelly slowed down. The bank was a brown brick structure sandwiched between a health-food store and a shop with hashish pipes displayed in its window. Kelly applied the brakes. He backed into a parking space and turned off the engine.

Carr opened the door and got out. LaMonica slid across the car seat and struggled, handcuffed, to pull himself out of the vehicle. Carr reached down and cupped the prisoner's elbow to assist. LaMonica sprang to his feet and slammed his handcuffed wrists into Carr's face. The agent fell backward onto the sidewalk, his eyes blinded by a stiletto of pain. LaMonica bolted. Kelly ran past, shouting. Carr's eyes came back into focus. He was on his feet and running down an alley next to the bank. The warmth of blood spread across his forehead. Wiping it off with his hand, he turned right and trotted quietly along the alley behind the shops. Kelly burst through a store's rear entrance and almost knocked him over. The agents bumped into one another running back in the door. It was a narcotics paraphernalia shop. The bearded man standing behind a cash register looked sheepish. Carr grabbed him by the collar and pulled him across the counter to within an inch of his bloody face. "Where *is* he, you son of a bitch?" The man's eyes rolled to a door at the other end of the store. Carr shoved him backward as Kelly yanked the door open. They rushed into a roomful of boxes. The only other door led to the street. It was ajar. They ran outside.

"Radio for help!" screamed an out-of-breath Carr. He continued his hunt up and down the street, in and out of stores, into alleys. Finally, he returned to the government sedan. Kelly barked instructions and a description to two uniformed officers. They jumped back in their cars and sped off in opposite directions. A car full of special agents arrived and divided into teams of two. Having pinned gold badges to their suit coats, they searched the storefronts on the opposite side of the street, running around like madmen.

CHAPTER 5

Linda Gleason flicked the television and the living room filled with the organ music leading to "The Days of Our Lives." She plopped down on the sofa. As soon as she found out whether Rex was returning to Samantha or flying off to Africa with Claudia, she would wash her hair. She lit a cigarette.

There was a casual knock on the door.

Probably Charlie Carr with the reward money, Linda thought. "Coming," she said. She jumped up and opened the door.

It was Paul, and his face was red. He punched her fully on the point of her chin. Her head hit the carpet. She wanted to scream, but couldn't. Was her jaw broken?

"Did you bail out?" she mumbled.

Ignoring her, he closed and locked the door. Violently, he pulled off his belt. His eyes were wide in anger. She vaulted off the carpet and ran into the bedroom. The night-stand phone was in her hand. She dialed *0*.

He was in the room. "You stabbed me in the back, you rat-bitch-snake, cunt, dirty bitch . . ."

"Operator," said a pleasant female voice. Something was around Linda Gleason's neck. She couldn't speak. It was his belt! The receiver dropped from her hand. No air. Her eyes felt as if they were popping out. She had this odd picture in her mind: her eyes and contact lenses actually popping completely out of her head and dropping on the carpet near the front door.

It had grown dark. The streetlights came on.

Carr sat on the fender of his sedan like a conductor without a train. Using a blood-spotted handkerchief, he dabbed for the hundredth time at the throbbing wound on his forehead. The last of the police officers had given up the search and departed. Across the street, the remaining Treasury agents piled into a G-car. The driver waved at him and drove off.

Carr was light-headed, thirsty, and slightly nauseous.

Jack Kelly wandered out of an alley down the block carrying something in his hand. "Looky here," he said before coming to a full stop. He handed Carr a pair of handcuffs with a key sticking out of one of the ratchet locks. Kelly pointed behind him. "Found 'em in the alley behind that coffee shop. Can you believe that sneaky bastard carrying a *handcuff key?* Talk about *planning ahead.* He must have had it in a shoe." The bearlike man was staring at Carr's forehead. "You're going to need stitches," he said.

"Not yet," Carr said. "I'll call Linda. We'll have to find a place for her to stay until we catch him." He dug a dime out of his pocket and made his way to a pay phone at a newsstand down the street. He dropped in the dime and dialed. The line was busy. He walked back to the car and got in.

Kelly started the engine. "Only you would think of a goddamn informant before yourself," he said, pulling the sedan into traffic.

Carr knocked on the door of Linda's apartment. The blinds were closed and there was no sound inside.

"She's not home," Kelly said. He jiggled change in his pants pocket.

Carr rang the doorbell. Still no answer. An older woman

wearing a floral-patterned housecoat and a turban of hair rollers shuffled out of the apartment next door. Her arms were folded across her chest. She stared at Carr's forehead. He opened his coat and displayed the badge on his belt. "Federal officers," he said. "Have you seen Miss Gleason?"

"She's in there," said the woman. "One of her many *boyfriends* was just over; he came and left in a taxicab."

Carr felt like someone had slugged him in the stomach with a baseball bat. He was in Korea again, shells bursting; soldiers were screaming. He grabbed the door handle and turned. It was unlocked. He pushed it open. Linda was lying in a fetal position in the middle of the living-room floor, her hands clutching a man's belt around her neck. Her face was ashen and her eyes open, staring. Carr dropped to his knees next to her.

"Holy mother of Christ," Kelly said. He crossed himself. Taking out a handkerchief, he reached for the phone on the coffee table.

"Use the car radio," Carr said.

Kelly rushed out the door.

With two fingers, Carr closed Linda's eyes. He traced the tiny crow's-feet. He pulled his hand away.

The woman in rollers edged in the door. Her hands flew to her face and she started to wail. Carr waved her back. She retreated like a wounded animal.

Carr felt cold. He rubbed his eyes for a moment. He was drained, exhausted after twenty years on the street.

Carr sat on the edge of a paper-covered examination table in the hospital's emergency room. Outside the room a nurse kept telling a sobbing child not to rub something or it would get worse. There was the smell of witch hazel. A young woman doctor with a nose that protruded almost as much as her ponytail stood in front of him holding a curved needle. She said, "This is going to hurt a little," as she took a stitch in his forehead. She was right.

Kelly barged in through a set of swinging doors. "La-Monica's key fit one of the safe-deposit boxes in the bank," he said, "but as I'm sure you've probably guessed by now, the box was empty."

"Don't move your head, dammit," the doctor said.

"Sorry," Carr mumbled.

"That LaMonica is a fast thinker," Kelly said. "He thought up that whole little act after we arrested him." He shook his head. "Who would have figured him to go straight back over to Linda's, though? Any normal crook would have hot-footed it out of town without looking back. But not LaMonica; the first thing that came to his mind was revenge. He's vicious, a real animal."

The doctor stuck the needle in again and Carr winced.

"I bet that smarts," Kelly said. "You look like death warmed over."

The doctor stopped sewing. She pointed the needle at Kelly. "Sir, would you mind getting the hell out of this room?"

Kelly raised his hands and backed out the door.

Paul LaMonica sat next to the window in the seat behind the bus driver. He rubbed his wrists. As the bus chugged along Hollywood Boulevard he felt anonymous, safe for the time being. He knew that cops did not stop buses to look for escapees.

The sight of a police radio car cruising next to the bus startled him. He stared down at the vehicle as if viewing an alligator from a jungle barge. The radio car turned onto a side street.

A half hour later, the bus pulled into the busy L.A. Airport traffic circle and inched along in the bumper-to-bumper crush. Finally it stopped. Paul LaMonica stepped off the crowded bus and smelled jet fuel. He blended into the bustling crowd heading for the international departures terminal. Inside, he stopped for a moment in front of a flight information screen and noted the departure gate number for a Paris-bound flight. He followed another crowd down a tiled corridor and up an escalator. At the top of the conveyance was a gift shop wedged next to a cocktail lounge. He strolled into the gift shop and purchased two newspapers and a cheap flight bag. After stuffing the papers into the bag, he zipped it up.

Casually he sauntered out of the gift shop and into the cocktail lounge. It was a dark place with a long bar and windows that faced the airport runway. Travelers of all ages huddled around the tables in the room. There were lots of clocks on the walls. LaMonica wound his way across the floor, surveying the patrons. Finally, he sat down at a table next to an auburn-haired woman of medium build. She was about his age and dressed in a conservative dark skirt and blouse. An enormous purse and an overnight case were in the chair next to her. The case had a Paris baggage tag.

When a young waitress approached, he ordered a straight soda. She returned with the drink and he paid. As she walked away, LaMonica hefted his glass to the woman sitting next to him. "Happy travels," he said with a fatherly wink.

The woman hesitated, then picked up her glass. "Same to you," she said. She sipped and set the glass down.

"Paris?" he said.

She nodded. "My first trip."

"You'll love Paris. It's a beautiful city. I'm a pilot. I fly there every other week. I'm going over today to pick up a flight."

"I just can't wait to get there. It's my first trip to Europe."

LaMonica smiled. Nothing was said for a while.

"Are the lines at the ticket counter always so long?" she asked.

"I'm afraid I wouldn't know. As a pilot I'm not required to check in at the ticket counter."

"Of course," she said in a slightly embarrassed tone.

"But I did see an extremely long line at the passport office. I'm lucky enough to have a friend who works there, so I just dropped off my passport. He told me he'd stamp it and I could pick it up just before departure time."

The woman's hands plunged into her purse. She pulled

out her passport. "A stamp?" she said as she flipped through the pages.

"It's a new requirement," he said. "A passport officer places a trip stamp on the last page of each passport. If one arrives in France without such a stamp, it causes nothing but problems."

The woman looked worried. "My travel agent didn't tell me. Where is the passport office?"

"It's right next to the pilots' check-in office," he said. "I'm on my way to pick up my passport right now. I'll be happy to show you the way."

"Thank you," the woman said. She struggled to pick up her luggage.

"If you'd like, I can have your passport stamped while I'm there. It'll save you carting all your luggage."

The woman furrowed her brow.

"And perhaps you'd be kind enough to keep an eye on my flight bag while I'm gone."

The woman hesitated for a moment. She gazed at the flight bag. "Uh, yes. That would be very kind."

LaMonica held out his hand and she gave him the passport. He stuffed it into his shirt pocket. "Be back in a few minutes." He went down the escalator and joined the crowd of travelers heading for the street. At a rental-car desk near the ticket counters, he used a credit card to rent a sedan. From the airport, he drove directly to a printing supply house on Sepulveda Boulevard and picked up the inks and bond paper he had ordered. Having loaded the items neatly into the trunk of the rented car, he drove to the San Diego freeway and headed south.

After stopping for lunch at a coffee shop, he entered a bank and purchased one $500-denomination traveler's check. Taking care not to fold it, he slipped the check into an envelope. Back on the freeway again, he went over the supply list in his mind. Unless he was wrong, he had everything he needed.

CHAPTER 6

So far, the interview was going pretty much as Carr had figured it would. After warning him of his rights, Special Agent in Charge Norbert Waeves, fortified behind a desk covered with nameplates, photo cubes, and pipe paraphernalia, had asked Carr to recount his activities for the entire day "in question" and followed up with an inquiry about how the case had originated. With each of Carr's answers, Waeves would make a little puff of pipe smoke and jot something down on his ever-present yellow notepad. A tape recorder sat on the desk between them like a large black magnet.

Waeves, a kinky-haired, freckled man who was a few years younger than Carr, held up his pencil like a dart. "Again," he said. "What time was it when the prisoner escaped?"

"About five," Carr replied. His eyes were on the wall behind the desk, where Waeves's framed headquarters commendation letters (the preprinted kind other agents threw away) and photographs of his gun collection were displayed.

"I'd like a more accurate estimate. Was it closer to after five or before five?" Waeves said. His smile was strained.

"Like I said, it was about five." Suddenly Carr realized what looked different about Waeves. It was the new suit. Shoulder pads.

"How do you *know* it was five?" Waeves insisted. "Why couldn't it have been four or six?"

"I don't know. I guess I looked at my watch." Carr frowned.

Waeves glanced at the yellow pad. He printed what looked like the word *five* and underlined it. He put the pen down. "So, you called for help and searched for the escaped prisoner," he said. "Then what?"

"We couldn't find him."

The interrogator nodded. "Go ahead."

"Go ahead what?"

"What did you do then?"

"I called the informant from a pay phone," Carr said. "Her line was busy."

"Why did you try to call her?"

"To tell her LaMonica had escaped."

"How do you know the line was busy? Couldn't the phone just as easily have been out of order?" Waeves made a sucking sound on the pipe.

Carr closed his eyes for a moment, then opened them. "Her line was busy so we drove over to her apartment."

"How long did it take?"

"To do what?"

"To drive to her apartment."

"Because of the rush-hour traffic it took about a half hour," Carr said.

"Would you say it was closer to twenty-five minutes or thirty-five minutes?"

"Yes."

"Yes, what?"

"It was about half an hour," Carr said.

Waeves's angular face became blotchy. He coughed nervously. "How long had Linda Gleason been your informant?"

"About five years."

"And how was she recruited?"

49

"She was a walk-in," Carr said. "Her husband was murdered on a contract let by Tony Dio the loan shark and she wanted to get even. She gave me enough information on one of Dio's hoods that I was able to get a search warrant for his house. I found fifty grand in tens and the weapon that was used on her husband inside the house. Headquarters authorized a cash payment to her after the conviction, and from then on she just kept feeding me information. She always worked as a cocktail waitress in one or the other of the local hood hangouts. They trusted her because her husband had a reputation for being solid. No one ever suspected her as far as I know." *You know the story as well as I do, you two-faced bastard.*

Waeves leaned back in his chair. He rolled a pen on the back of his knuckles. "You arrested LaMonica at the informant's apartment, leaving no doubt as to her role as the informant," he said. "What is your explanation for this tactic?"

"It was her idea," Carr said. "She felt comfortable with the scenario and I accepted that." Carr was talking to the recorder. He knew the tape would be played like a party record by the inspectors in Washington, D.C. "Linda Gleason was an active, longtime informant whose original revenge motivation had turned into a financial one. She got a few extra bucks now and then for doing nothing more than repeating bar talk. She had provided information on at least forty cases. It was common for her to make up the scenario for her undercover role."

The recorder squeaked. The tape had run out. Waeves punched the "eject" button with a bony finger and the cassette popped out. He yanked open the desk drawer and rummaged around for a fresh cassette.

"You don't have anything on me," Carr said. "My operation will be ruled 'in policy.'"

Waeves slammed the drawer shut and opened another. He moved things around. "We'll see," he said.

"Take your best shot, pencil pusher," Carr said.

Waeves pulled a cassette out of the drawer and stuffed it into the machine as if plugging a dike.

Carr's tone changed to one of courtesy. "Are there any other questions, Mr. Waeves?" He was looking at the tape recorder.

"Yes," said the blotchy-faced man. "What time was it when . . ."

It was after 9:00 P.M. by the time Carr arrived at Ling's bar. He pushed aside a portal of hanging beads and looked around for his partner. Ling's, like the other haunts in Chinatown, was kept mysteriously dark. Bar jokes had it that the cavelike atmosphere was due to Ling's desire to save on utility bills, but Carr suspected that the detectives who drank there preferred the lack of light.

Kelly waved, drink in hand, from a bar-stool perch facing the door. Carr made his way to him and sat down.

Ling, wearing his usual bow tie and long-sleeved white shirt, wiped his wire-framed eyeglasses on his sleeve. He put them back on. "Charlie," he said, grabbing a Scotch bottle. He poured a drink and set it down in front of Carr. "Lady sheriff detective ask about you last night. Big blonde," he whispered. "She want to know if I have your address since you transfer back. I thought maybe I give her my address. Maybe get her in bed with me and lay her before she know what happens!" He gave a high-pitched laugh.

Carr smiled and shook his head.

Still laughing, Ling poured more drinks and rushed to the other end of the bar.

"How long did he have you in his office?" Kelly said.

"About two hours."

"Same here," Kelly said. "Christ, you'd think *we'd* killed Linda." He shook his head sadly.

"That's just the way he is," Carr said.

Kelly set his drink down. "You're right there. He's the same pipe-smoking, ass-kissing, *i*-dotting mama's boy bureaucrat he always was. Over the years I've had dreams about kicking the shit out of him. Literally pounding his fuggin' head in."

"I know what you mean," Carr said. He gulped fully

51

half of the Scotch-and-water and put the glass down. Neither man said anything for a while.

"Linda was getting careless," Kelly said. "She'd done too many cases. She shouldn't have brought the guy over to her apartment. It was a stupid thing to do."

"She had a lot of guts."

"We don't have anything to go on," Kelly said. "LaMonica could be anywhere by now."

"We'll find him," Carr said after a while. "And when we do we're going to play catch-up."

Carr and Kelly spent the next day standing around in the hallway outside Judge Malcolm's courtroom waiting to testify. The case was a leftover that predated Carr's transfer to Washington. Because of assorted technicalities, Judge Malcolm had granted twelve defense motions for continuance in almost two years. Carr wasn't particularly surprised by the delay because he had seen the defense lawyer use the same strategy in other cases.

At 4:00 P.M., Assistant U.S. Attorney Reba Partch, a harried young woman with thick glasses, wiry hair, and an oversized rear end, strode out of the courtroom. She wore a black velvet jacket with a matching tie and a huge dandruffy collar. "You two are excused," she said gruffly. "I let him plead to one count for straight probation." She dug a package of cough drops out of her jacket and popped a couple into her mouth. "It's a weak case anyway, and I'm sick of making court appearances on it. There've been a million continuances. Even the judge is sick of the case." She maneuvered the cough drops around in her mouth.

Kelly's face reddened. "Since when is a confession a weak case?" he said. "He *told* us he did it. Not to mention the fact that he had a stack of phony twenties in his pocket when we arrested him. The jerk has a record a mile long."

"If we went to trial on him and lost, then what would we have?" she said.

"The same thing we have right now," Kelly said. "Nothing."

Her tongue arranged the cough drops so she could speak.

"You people are completely out of touch with reality," she said, cough drops rattling against her teeth. She flung open the door and hustled back into the courtroom.

Kelly was still talking about the incident that night as he drove south past fog-shrouded motels and fast-food stands along the Pacific Coast Highway, a two-lane road that wound through the beach cities. "Her daddy raised her, paid for her law school, and juiced her way into the federal prosecutor's job with a nice fat political contribution. The only thing he couldn't do for her was try her cases."

"You don't become a judge by taking cases to trial," Carr said. "You might lose. Sally told me that Judge Malcolm never tried a case during his days as prosecutor. He had a perfect record when he was appointed to the bench."

"I don't want to talk about it anymore," Kelly said as he swung the G-car into a parking lot next to a smallish building. A flashing marquee on its roof proclaimed "Shorty McFadden's—Le Jazz Club." They got out of the car and strolled to the rear door of the place. The sound of a saxophone came from inside. Both men tightened their belts to keep their guns from bulging under their suit jackets. Carr opened the door and they went inside.

Blue lights shone through cigarette smoke onto a stage that barely had room enough for the combo on it. Shorty McFadden, a fragile-looking, jockey-sized man wearing a French-cut white suit and a black turtleneck, was playing a fiery "Cherokee" on his sax. As he harmonized, his eyes were half shut and his knees bent with the rhythm. He had thinning brown hair and the chalky complexion of a man who had just been released from solitary confinement.

The crowd was mixed: beach types, a few blacks, more than a few middle-aged hoods with young women, some sunken-cheeked hypes. The T-men were the focus of lots of stares, including one from a black woman bartender with corn-rowed hair who was as tall as a basketball player. Carr and Kelly took a seat at a corner table that provided a view of both doors.

At the end of the set, Shorty McFadden bowed to the applause and told the audience in a hoarse voice that it was time for a break. He set the saxophone on its stand and lit a cigarette. Then he hopped off the stage and wound his way to the bar, shaking hands along the way. The Amazon bartender said something to him and he headed straight for Carr's table. Everyone shook hands. Shorty greeted the T-men without smiling. Come to think of it, Carr had never seen him smile. The diminutive man pulled up a chair.

"Is there anything going on in here?" McFadden asked, sounding concerned.

"Nothing like that," Carr said. "We just stopped by to talk."

"If you ever get word that anything is going on in here, just tell me. I'll burn whoever it is right then and there. I've put the word out that nothing goes down in Shorty's. My old lady had to go to six hearings before the liquor board granted her a license for this place. I will burn *anyone* who brings trouble in here. I didn't spend fifteen years bouncing from San Quentin to Lexington with a needle sticking out of my arm so that some punk could do business in my club and get the place shut down. This place is my *dream*, man." He puffed on his cigarette. Smoke wafted out of his mouth and into his nose. "In the old days I used to wake up in the morning and gulp a handful of uppers. During the day I'd use heroin, numorphan, sleeping pills, and drink a gallon of wine. Sometimes I'd lay down about five A.M. or so and try to catch a few winks. And, even with all that shit in my system, do you know what was on my mind? The idea of someday owning my own jazz club . . . of being able to get up on a stage like I just did and blow 'Cherokee' for my friends. Well, I finally got my dream. And if anybody does anything to fuck it up, even though I'm a solid guy who went to the joint more than once because I wouldn't hand up my friends, I'll burn 'em." He finished off a cigarette with a puff that fired paper all the way back to the filter, and blew out the smoke.

"I need some background information," Carr said.

Shorty McFadden lit a fresh cigarette. He puffed once and coughed once. "Shoot."

"Teddy Mora," Carr said.

"The Teddy Mora I know deals paper out of the Castaways Lounge one day of the week," McFadden said. "The rest of the time he's hard to find. I heard he just bought a head shop down the street from Grauman's Chinese. I met him once in the U.S. marshal's lockup when I was awaiting trial. We both made bail at the same time. He had some bank counter-checks and I downed 'em. I gave him front money for some more, and he never came through. He's a snake, a back-stabber."

"Have you ever heard the name *Paul LaMonica?*" Carr said.

Shorty nodded. "He's a paper pusher too . . . funny money and checks. But when I was hanging paper, I never scored from him. The word was that if you crossed him he'd kill ya. Not just get pissed off, but actually blow you away. I wasn't real big on the idea of ending up in the refrigerator because I shortened him five bucks in buy money or some shit. We were in the same cell block at Terminal Island for a while. He choked a Mexican to death with a rolled-up sheet and got away with it. Even the usual snitches refused to testify against him. He's the kind of guy who would figure out a way to transfer to another joint just to get you. The word is that he learned how to print . . . does his own paper now and sells it. He's screwy, a loner."

"We need some help in finding him," Carr said. "He's a fugitive."

With a cigarette hanging out of his mouth, McFadden slowly shook his head. "Four years ago you grabbed me redhanded in a bank. My wife was dying in the County Hospital. When you took me to see her before you booked me, it was the first time a cop had done a favor for me. I said it then and I'll say it now, I'll tell you anything you want to know." He pointed to his temple. "What's up here is yours for the asking, but I'll never set anybody up and I'll never testify. If I did, I would be a rat. And no one likes a rat. So if you're asking me to find the man and set him up for you, the answer is no. I'm not a snitch."

The lady bartender carried a tray over to them. She set a full bottle of expensive Scotch and two glasses of ice on the table. Her complexion was deep African black and she had wide lips, hips, and cheekbones. She wore gypsy earrings.

"This is my new old lady," McFadden said. He introduced Carr and Kelly by their first names. "These people are friends. Take care of them when they come in."

The woman winked and walked back to the bar.

"We met at a methadone treatment center," McFadden said. "That woman has changed my life. She won't even let me drink." He picked up the bottle and filled their glasses.

"Is there anything else you can tell me about LaMonica?" Carr said.

Shorty McFadden started to light a cigarette but realized he already had one in the ashtray. He stuffed it back in the pack. "He has a missing finger," he said. "As the story goes, he was running off a load of hundreds in a cabin up near Big Bear Lake and he got his finger caught in the printing press. He was alone, and of course he couldn't holler for help. He ended up chopping his own finger off." Shorty McFadden shook his head. "If it was me, I think I would rather have just started yelling and taken the trip back to the joint for a deuce or so." He glanced at the stage. The other musicians had hopped on it and were picking up their instruments. Shorty McFadden snapped his fingers and pointed at Carr. "Rosemary," he said. "The broad who used to forge all the stolen savings bonds. She knows LaMonica. I suggest you talk with her. She might be able to do you some good."

"What's her last name?" Kelly said.

"Clamp or Clump or something like that," McFadden said.

"Where do we find her?" Carr asked.

"The last I heard, she was running an art gallery on Melrose right near the Beverly Hills city limit. As I understand it, she doesn't do savings bonds anymore because every forgery bull in L.A. knows her handwriting by sight." Shorty McFadden smiled for the first time. Carr thought his face looked like a yellow rubber mask. Maybe it was just the lighting . . .

Shorty McFadden glanced at his wristwatch. "What would you like to hear?" he said.

"How about 'I Can't Get Started With You,'" Carr said.

"You got it." Shorty McFadden stood up and sauntered through the crowd, shaking hands. Then he climbed onto the stage, picked up his saxophone, and tested the mouthpiece. He nodded at the bass man and began to blow.

After the first tune, Carr and Kelly finished their drinks and slipped out the back door. Thick fog had rolled in. They climbed into the G-car. Kelly turned on the headlights and started the engine. He drove down an alley lined with trash cans and through a service-station lot. A pickup truck behind them took the same route. Kelly turned north on the Pacific Coast Highway and stepped on the gas. A few blocks later he made a right turn onto a residential street. The pickup truck did the same.

"Somebody's on our ass," Kelly said.

"I see him," Carr said. The truck pulled up within a few feet of their rear bumper. The headlights blinked on and off.

"This is as good a place as any," Carr said, as he dug around in the glove compartment. Having found a flashlight, he reached for his gun.

Kelly slowed down and pulled over to the curb. He yanked his revolver out. The pickup stopped a car-length or so behind them and the headlights went out. In the gray illumination of a lone streetlight, he saw the figure of a man with long black hair exit the truck. Slowly, the man headed for the passenger side of the sedan.

"Now!" Carr said. The Treasury men swung open the doors of the car and jumped out, pistols drawn.

The man raised his hands. "It's me, Frank Garcia!" he said, his hands reaching higher. "Easy does it."

Carr shone the flashlight in Garcia's face. The T-men put their guns away.

Garcia lowered his hands. "I saw you coming out the back door at Shorty's," he said as he walked closer. "We've had him under surveillance for a week."

"What's he in to?" Carr said.

"He's the Mr. Big in a five-pound white heroin deal," Garcia said. He had a barrio accent. "Delivery is expected any day."

"You must have the wrong guy," Carr said, smiling. "Shorty just told us he's finally cleaned up his act."

"He's cleaned up all right," Garcia said. "I've made two buys from him and three from his bitch within the last week. They're dealing China white out of the place like they had a license. The load he's waiting for is one he financed himself. He made a down payment on a fishing boat and hired a couple of stooges to make a round trip to Acapulco. They're on their way back right now. As soon as the heroin is delivered, we're going to take him and his old lady off. I figured you might want to know."

"Thanks for the tip," Carr said.

"See you down at Ling's," Garcia said. He trotted back to the pickup truck, climbed in, and used the microphone. As he drove off, he gave a wave.

"Maybe you should have requested Shorty to play 'Goodnight Irene,'" Kelly said. They both laughed.

CHAPTER 7

It was almost 2:00 A.M.

Charles Carr drove out of Chinatown onto the Santa Monica freeway heading toward his apartment. He was full of booze, chicken-roll hors d'oeuvres, and cop talk. Stopping off at Sally Malone's was something he hadn't consciously planned on doing; maybe it was the liquor or the empty morning streets of the tepid Santa Ana wind swirling in the open windows that brought him there.

Having parked the car, he shuffled up the steps to her apartment. He knocked gently on the door, waited awhile, and knocked again.

"Who is it?" Sally said.

Suddenly Carr wished he hadn't come. Could he just trot down the steps and drive off?

Sally Malone opened the door a few inches. "Charlie!" She turned on the light in the apartment.

"I've had a few drinks," he said. "I didn't realize it was so late." As soon as the words were out of his mouth, he realized how utterly lame they sounded.

Sally stepped back from the door. "Come on in before you wake up my gossipy neighbors," she whispered. She was wearing a terrycloth bathrobe that stopped way above

59

her knees. Since he'd last seen her she had cut her chestnut hair into a stylish curly shag. The change made her look younger than her forty years.

He walked in and Sally closed the door behind him. *"Well,"* she said, going to the stove and lighting a burner under a coffeepot.

He followed her into the kitchen. Like the rest of the well-furnished apartment, it was immaculate. "I'd just as soon have a beer if you don't mind," he said.

She shook the coffeepot and set it down. "Nice of you to find the time to stop by," she said.

He stared at the kitchen floor for a moment. Sally Malone didn't look up from the stove. Carr opened the refrigerator door and took out a beer. Avoiding eye contact, she grabbed a bottle opener off the counter and handed it to him. He popped the cap. "I've been busy since I got back . . . been meaning to give you a ring."

They both watched the fire under the coffeepot for a moment. "All moved in to your apartment?" she said.

"Right," he said. "Same building as before. I guess I'm a creature of habit."

She picked up the coffeepot and poured. "I'm not," she said without any hint of a smile. "My life has changed since you were transferred. I'm into lots of new and interesting things; lots of meetings. I'm active in a jogging club, a women's rights group, the steno association . . . nothing you'd be interested in, of course, but I'm busier than I ever have been in my life. It's satisfying. I've found that I thrive on activity."

"How's the activity at the FBI?" Carr said. He swigged his beer.

After a long silence, Sally spoke to the stove. "I went out with Tom Luegner a few times, if that's what you're referring to," she said. "He's a complete jerk. All he does is talk about his silver fifty-coats-of-lacquer Corvette, or his precious informants, whom he refers to mysteriously as 'Alpha one twenty-three' or 'Delta sixty-seven.' As if I really cared. He lives a big FBI-top-secret act to impress everyone."

Almost gently, Carr put the beer down on the sink. "I'd better go," he said, running his hands through his hair. "It's three in the morning and I've been drinking. I'm out of line sliding over here uninvited, and it's none of my business who you go out with. Let's just say I dropped over to say hello to an old pal." His hand touched her cheek softly. She threw her arms around him. They hugged, and Sally pressed her head to his chest.

"I'm going to go," Carr said.

"I've missed you so much," Sally said. "I waited for you to call me."

"Ah, I don't like to talk on the phone," Carr said. Another lame remark.

Sally spoke with her head still buried in his chest. "You're going to stay here tonight and we're going to make love until we"—she giggled—"break into a sweat, as you used to call it." She threw her head back and looked him in the eye. "Do you remember the time you said that to me?" She put her head back on his chest before he had to answer. "It was our first weekend together. I still remember. It was almost nine years ago."

In the bedroom they helped each other undress. "If we use each other, then so be it," she said. They took turns making love to one another. Their bodies meshed and twisted, and Carr felt her familiar smooth thighs under, on top, and around him. Their kisses became bites. Finally they rested.

At daybreak Carr woke up and crawled out of bed. In the semidarkness he found his clothes and dressed. Sally stirred.

Carrying his shoes, Carr tiptoed out the bedroom door. As he closed it, he thought he heard Sally say "Bastard!"

Paul LaMonica tapped the accelerator and inched forward in a snake of cars. To his right was a large green sign: YOU ARE LEAVING THE UNITED STATES. He rolled down the window of the rented sedan and let in a swirling breeze that Mexicans would recognize as a portent of a Baja rainstorm. A San Diego police van sat parked next to the sign, rear doors open and waiting. The crew-cut prisoners huddled inside looked like sailors on leave.

A guard booth less than fifty yards ahead was manned by a Mexican policeman wearing what looked like a bus driver's uniform with a gun belt and holster. LaMonica looked at his wristwatch and took a deep breath. The breeze made his hands feel clammy on the steering wheel, though he knew that logically there was nothing to worry about at this point. Even if a border lookout were in effect, the slob policeman wouldn't have received notice yet. Besides, the only picture the feds had of him was three years old. If he was lucky, maybe they hadn't even *found* her body yet, and there was certainly no law against transporting printing supplies into Mexico. He would cross the border and be safe.

The lines of vehicles moved closer, and the policeman waved him forward. LaMonica took another deep breath and pulled ahead. "Wait," the policeman said, fumbling for something in his trouser pockets. LaMonica noticed that the officer needed a shave. Without changing his somber expression, the policeman stepped backward into the guard booth and opened a drawer. LaMonica felt piano wires cinch tightly around his forehead. His foot felt magnetized to the accelerator.

The cop pulled a white card out of the drawer. He stepped out of the booth and handed it to LaMonica. It read:

CLUB DISCO

GIRLS GIRLS GIRLS

THIS COUPON GOOD FOR ONE FREE DRINK

On the reverse of the card was a crude map of downtown Tijuana marked with an *X*. "Here is where you find what you want," said the cop.

"*Gracias,*" LaMonica said. His throat was dry. The policeman waved him on.

• • •

LaMonica drove along a highway that followed the northern edge of Tijuana. He followed the signs to Ensenada. After a while he crossed a bridge over a wide gully cluttered with huts made of cardboard and scrap lumber; makeshift homes that would be washed away with the first rain.

The road ahead was clear. LaMonica felt tired, daydreamy. The memory of his first arrest often came back to him when he was feeling this way. He had been sitting in his car across the street from the bank. A talk show was on the radio. "My son keeps things hidden from me," a woman whined. "He screams at me every time I go into his room. I think he's afraid I'll see him naked." The woman's voice was probing, headachy, like his mother's. The talk-show host was Dr. Robert C. Mendenhall the radio counselor, L.A.'s "Voice of Health."

He had turned off the radio in the middle of Mendenhall's advice and climbed out of the car. Pulling the briefcase out of the trunk, he marched straight into the bank.

Inside the air-conditioned lobby, he waited his turn in a long line in front of a window marked "Commercial Accounts." Oddly, he wasn't the least bit nervous. Finally, he reached the window. The bespectacled woman behind the counter had bluish-gray hair and wore a buttoned-to-the-neck suit of the same color.

"I own the car lot down the street," he said as he snapped open the briefcase. He dumped the rubber-banded stacks of ten-dollar bills on the counter. "An elderly couple just bought a Mercedes and paid for it in *cash*. Can you believe that?" He chuckled.

The woman's face was expressionless. Like a robot, she pulled off the rubber bands and counted the bills. With each stack, she made a mark on a little white pad. "Is this for deposit?" she said without looking up.

"I'd like the whole amount in hundred-dollar bills. I'm going to an antique-automobile auction tonight. The purchases are all in cash, but I'd rather just carry a nice neat little bundle of hundreds than—"

"I don't have that many hundred-dollar bills," she interrupted. "I'll have to go get some out of the vault." She opened her cash drawer and set the tens inside it. Using a key she removed from her pocket, she locked the drawer. She shuffled into the vault.

He was still waiting at the teller window when the police arrived.

The woman pointed a finger at him (her lack of expression even when doing this was remarkable). The policeman twisted his arms behind his back. The handcuffs clicked on. "Those tens have been on the warning list for over a month," he heard her say. The cops dragged him out the front door of the bank. He went to trial and then to prison. It was the first time.

Never again, he'd promised himself on that day, would he make such a mistake. In the future he would weigh risks and attempt to control variables as carefully as a test pilot would.

The road wound around a hill crowned with shacks and finally led down past the turnoff for the bullring by the sea. With the first whiff of salt air LaMonica felt secure again, safe from those who would put him back in prison clothes.

In less than an hour he reached Ensenada. The town proper comprised a collection of kitschy hotels and souvenir shops accordioned together. Like other cities on the U.S. border, the town lived off camper-truck travelers in cowboy hats, sports-car types, and college kids looking for a cheap weekend.

LaMonica pulled up at a stop sign. Across the street a newly built sports-betting office overlooked a dry riverbed where brown children played with empty pop bottles. The light turned green. He drove out of Ensenada and along a road that followed the coast.

At a clump of trees, LaMonica turned onto a dirt road and continued until he was fully within sight of a one-story, wood-frame house. The structure's sheet-metal roof glistened with sea-level heat. He stopped the car. Using binoculars, he watched the house for a few minutes. There was no activity, no sign that anything had been disturbed. He put the binoculars down and continued on.

In a swirl of red dust, LaMonica pulled up in front of the cabin, which the Mexican realtor who'd sold it to him had described as a beach house. He got out of the car and stretched. From the trunk, he unloaded cardboard boxes filled with reams of paper and ink cans. Having carted them to the door, he used a key to unfasten a large padlock. Inside, the air was oven temperature and smelled like printer's ink.

LaMonica flipped the light switch. In the middle of the room an offset printing press rested next to a worktable. Above it, a fluorescent light fixture hung from a rafter. Under the table, gallon bottles of printing chemicals were lined up exactly as he had left them. Next to the press a lithographic camera covered by a bedsheet loomed like an apparition. A darkroom fashioned out of tarp and lumber protruded from the wall. Beside it, a pillow rested on a canvas folding cot.

LaMonica pulled the sheet off the man-sized camera and used it to wipe off the lens. He paused for a moment to stare at his reflection: fair features; whitish hair one could describe as "distinguished"; firm biceps; the eyes and hands of a technician, a scientist, a man patient enough to endure prison—one whose symbol could be the forged and tempered steel that was the material of daggers.

Rummaging among his box of "Priority One" supplies —printers' manuals, color charts, half-tone screens, aluminum offset printing plates, lithographic film—LaMonica finally found an electric fan. He pulled it out of the box and plugged it in.

With the fan blowing on his sweaty frame, he took off his clothes and piled them on a chair. Naked, he was finally ready to get down to business. He sat at the table and resumed work on the passport. Using a razor blade, he separated the cover from the pages. He held a page up to the light. It had neither stamp marks nor folds. The bluish American eagle design, with its fine, unending lines of color, was pristine. He tossed the other pages under the table and began the work of mounting the pattern page for his copy camera. He accomplished this task as he did the rest of his printing efforts, without regard to time.

By early afternoon the heat in the workshop had become more than stifling. For a respite, LaMonica stepped in front of the fan and allowed the air to blow-dry his perspiration-soaked chest, genitals, and underarms. This refreshment was followed by a long drink from the jug of bottled water he had brought along. He repeated the process often.

By midnight the passport pages were printed and dried. Carefully he trimmed each page on a paper cutter and rounded the corners. He stapled them inside the cover. From a briefcase he removed a photograph of the peasant-cheeked Sandy Hartzbecker. She was posed leaning back against a wall with one knee up. She was nude except for a halter top. She had a cigarette in one hand and a cocktail glass in the other. With the paper cutter, he sliced away everything in the photograph except her head and shoulders. Using glue and a wipe rag, he affixed the photo-graph to the inside cover of the passport. This process alone took almost two hours.

Exhausted, LaMonica flicked off the light. He pulled the sheet off the litho camera and flopped down on the cot. Having covered himself, he closed his tired eyes. Before falling asleep, he imagined fucking Linda the cocktail waitress and then killing her and running naked across spikes and jagged chunks of glass without sustaining in-jury.

It was light outside when LaMonica woke up. He ate the contents of a can of peaches and drank the juice, then threw himself back into work.

Having mounted the traveler's check on a piece of card-board in front of the copy camera, he snapped photo after photo. Because of his precise standards, it took him almost three hours to prepare suitable negatives. Finally he held the completed black transparencies up to the fluorescent light and checked closely for flaws.

By eleven o'clock the cabin was sweltering. He flung open the door and stepped out onto the porch, shielding his eyes from the bright sunlight. Below the hills in the direction of town he could see the coastline and a procession of fishing boats heading toward the docks near the Ensenada fish market. Birds fluttered among the branches of a nearby tree. He picked up a rock and hurled it into the branches. The birds flew away. He stepped back into the cabin, tossed his clothing on the floor, and returned to work.

Using a grayish opaquing fluid and a fine-tipped brush, LaMonica painstakingly eradicated the signatures on the negative for the front of the traveler's check. By the time this procedure was completed, he had a stiff neck. Finally the negatives were ready. One at a time he arranged them on a vacuum-frame table and matched them to a thin lithographic printing plate that was about the size of a legal tablet. He fished around in his box of supplies and brought out a stopwatch. He flicked on an arc light and the stopwatch simultaneously and timed the plate exposures. In less than an hour the plates were completed.

After washing each of the plates in developing solution until the image of the checks was visible, he chose the ones he liked best and tossed the others on the floor. Without hesitation, he affixed the front plate onto the printing press and locked it into position. He took the time to carefully adjust the ink and water levels on the printing press, then flicked the "on" switch and stepped back. The sound of a press starting up gave him a slight chill (as it always had ever since the day he lost his finger).

The press worked efficiently, spitting perfect copies of the purple traveler's check into its basket. As reams were completed, LaMonica gingerly refilled the paper feed. After a couple of hours, stacks of counterfeit traveler's checks were piled up all over the cabin. Although fatigued, LaMonica took special care as he used a paper cutter to trim the traveler's checks. While doing this, he would occasionally compare one of the counterfeits with the genuine item to make sure it was the right size.

By 5:00 P.M. the job was completed. Having banded the checks, he stacked them in a large black briefcase. He carried the case to the car and locked it in the trunk.

Using a shovel and pick he had brought with him, he spent the next two hours digging a hole next to a tree near the cabin. He dragged the printing press out of the cabin and shoved it into the hole. He did the same with the copy camera and the vacuum frame. He covered the hole with dirt and returned to the cabin.

Using a two-gallon can of gasoline he kept on hand for emergencies, he doused the walls and floor as he backed out the front door. He lit a book of matches and tossed it into the room. A fire jumped. Paul LaMonica climbed in behind the wheel of the rented sedan and watched the cabin as it was engulfed in flames. He remembered the sound of fire engines arriving in front of his house when he was a child . . . and his mother's whining, sirenlike voice. *"I just don't know what to dooooooooooooooooooo with him,"* she'd said. He started the engine and drove off. As he cruised along the two-lane road toward Ensenada, the sun finally set. He was exhausted. Having taken a few deep breaths, he turned the car radio to a San Diego station. Suddenly an old man on a bicycle pulled into the roadway. Without slowing down, LaMonica swerved and missed him by a couple of feet. His heart beat rapidly for a few moments, then returned to normal.

CHAPTER 8

Kelly parked the government sedan in front of a small shop with a bright yellow awning mounted over a display window. The awning's calligraphic lettering announced "The New Life Gallery." Kelly followed Carr out of the sedan. They strolled to the window, which contained kaleidoscopic photographs of pasty-faced, embracing women. The photographs were flanked by a wooden box containing a pile of what appeared to be dyed red sand in the middle of a collection of kitchen knives. An artist's business card leaning against the wooden box bore the title "Women's Work."

Carr opened the door and stepped into the art gallery. There was the sound of a chime. A fortyish woman with close-cropped blond-streaked hair wearing a shapeless dress stood in the corner speaking softly with a pair of designer-jeaned women of similar age. Both had potbellies like half footballs, wore an excess of turquoise jewelry, and stood poised on six-inch heels. The woman in the shapeless dress acknowledged the agents with a nod and continued her conversation.

Kelly nudged Carr. He pointed to a pedestal next to the wall. Resting on it was a carved wood vagina lined with feathers and seashells. In the orifice, the artist had pasted a magazine photograph of women marching with banners. The price tag on the sculpture was $2,000. A mobile hanging above the sculpture was formed with photographs of female buttocks and love poems hand-lettered on Kotex.

After a few minutes, the potbellied women departed. The woman with the blond-streaked hair approached Carr and Kelly. Carr reached into his pocket for his badge.

"You don't have to show me anything," the woman said. "I can tell you're cops."

"Are you Rosemary Clamp?" Carr said.

"Cramp," she said. "Rosemary Cramp. But my name is now Rosanna DuMaurier. I had my name changed legally." Kelly continued to stare at the wooden sculpture. "It's the artist's self-portrait," she said.

Kelly nodded dumbly.

"We're looking for Paul LaMonica," Carr said.

"I don't know anyone anymore," she said. "I haven't been arrested for over five years. Of course you've probably checked my record and you already know that. Who told you that I knew Paul LaMonica?"

"We didn't come here to cause you any problems," Carr said. "We have a warrant for LaMonica's arrest and we're talking to a lot of people trying to find him." He looked her in the eye as he spoke.

"I don't appreciate you people coming into my gallery. It's totally uncalled for. I actually got a chill down my spine when I saw you walk in. I's like a reflex from my past life. I haven't been in trouble for over five years and I'm fully within my rights to ask you to get the hell out of here right now. Now, will you please *leave!* I mean it."

"I apologize if we've embarrassed you," Carr said. He nodded at an amazed Kelly and sauntered toward the door. He stopped in front of a rack of crude pencil drawings and sorted through them. He picked one up which depicted two disconsolate women sitting on a four-poster bed stroking a cat. He stared at the drawing for a moment. "How much is this?"

The woman gave him a searching look before speaking.

"Twenty-five dollars." Carr walked toward her with the drawing. He handed it to her and reached for his wallet. He pulled out some bills and gave them to her. The woman stared at the money for a moment, then accepted it.

"A cop buying lesbian art?" she said.

"It's a birthday present for my twin sister. She lives in San Francisco. We lead very different lives, but I respect her more than anyone I know. She had the courage to come out . . . to be honest." Carr turned and headed toward the door. He opened it.

"Do you remember the phony series E bonds that were cashed in the banks along Wilshire Boulevard five years ago?" said the woman.

Carr stepped back in and turned to face her. "Three grand's worth in every bank from downtown Los Angeles to Santa Monica. I remember the case well."

The woman tapped her chest. "Me," she said. "I can tell you now because the statute has run out and I can't be prosecuted."

"It was one of the best bond capers I've ever seen," Carr said. "Four agents spent weeks working on it. All we came up with was a vague description of a woman."

"I wore different wigs," she said. "Paul LaMonica was waiting in the car for me outside each bank. I ended up with nothing more than a few bucks out of the deal. There were too many people that had to be pieced off. Hell, at the time LaMonica was supplying my smack habit and that's all I really cared about. It was right after that caper that I got busted for marks and ended up doing a year in Frontera. I did a lot of thinking when I was in. For the first time in my life I admitted to my true sexuality. For the first time I realized that all of life is based on sex. Admitting my true nature solved virtually all of my problems. For once, I could accept myself. After I was released I kept completely away from the old crowd. I began living a new life. That's why I named this place the New Life Gallery.'

"Have you seen LaMonica in the past few months?" Carr said.

"He stops by once in a while when he's out of the joint.

He always wants me to do some phony paper for him, and I always shine him on."

"Any idea where I could find him?" Carr said.

"What did he do?"

"Escaped from Terminal Island."

"I'm sure you're already aware that all the paper pushers hang out at the Castaways Lounge in Hollywood," she said.

Carr nodded. "I've checked. He's not around there."

"Then I don't know what to tell you. But please, don't come around here anymore. My clientele is frightened of police types. This is more than just an art gallery. To my sisters and me, this is a shrine to women. The art here is a declaration of sexual truth. As a matter of fact, I believe that not being honest with oneself is the root cause of drug addiction. I know that my own problem disappeared as soon as I came out." She plucked a bread-dough plaque of buttocks and breasts off the wall and dusted it on her dress. She rehung it. "It's been a long journey for me, but I've finally arrived. If you people would have knocked on my door a few years ago, I would have jumped through any available window. I was involved in so many crimes that when I was questioned by the cops I had to be told which crime they were talking about in order to confess." She shook her head and smiled.

"Did LaMonica phone you a couple of days ago?" Carr said.

"Who told you that?"

"What did he want?"

"As usual he wanted me to do a deal with him. He offered me half of the action, said all I had to do was play a part. I assumed it was some kind of a con scheme."

"Did he give you any details?"

"Paul LaMonica doesn't give details. With him, everything is on a need-to-know basis. Had I agreed to come in, he would have waited until the last minute to fill me in on the details, names, and places. He believes in high security. That's all I'm going to say."

"Thanks." Carr turned toward the door.

"Is your sister really one of us?" she asked.

Carr nodded. "Yes," he said in a tone of sincerity. "And I *am* very proud of her." He walked out the door. Kelly followed.

The agents climbed in the G-car. Kelly got behind the wheel and started the engine. "I say, *lez-be-on-our-way,*" Kelly said. He laughed uproariously. *"My twin sister in San Francisco!"* He laughed again and Carr joined in. Kelly caught his breath. "I almost had a heart attack trying not to crack up in there! You definitely should get the Bullshitter of the Year award for that act." He threw his head back and laughed again.

Carr took out his notepad and made some brief entries concerning the interview. He put the pad away. "Do you think she was holding back?"

"Hard to say."

Carr rubbed his hands through his hair. "If LaMonica was going to print counterfeit money, why would he call Rosemary and ask her to 'play a part'?"

"It doesn't make sense," Kelly said. As they drove down Melrose toward the Hollywood freeway, neither man spoke. Kelly signaled, then steered onto a freeway on ramp and accelerated. "I wonder who would pay two thousand dollars for a wood carving of a cunt?" he said.

Carr shrugged.

"The boss'll be here any minute," said the bearded man standing behind a glass display case filled with cutting mirrors, roach clips, glass beakers, and tiny scales. "He stops by once a week to pick up the till."

"We'll wait," Carr said.

Kelly was busy examining a book he had picked off a wall rack entitled *How to Grow Marijuana Indoors*. He slammed it back on the rack. Two teenage girls carrying schoolbooks came in the door and wandered over to a display of hollowed-out silver dollars and fake soda cans with secret compartments. They giggled. One nudged the other and nodded at the red-faced, staring Kelly. They giggled again and hurried out the door.

There was the sound of a car pulling up in the alley. A prune-faced man with a sharp chin and elbows shuffled in the back door. The clerk whispered to him. He turned around and faced the T-men. "I'm Teddy Mora," he said gravely. "You people looking for me?" He spun a ring of car keys lewdly around his middle finger.

Carr held out his gold badge. "A prisoner escaped yesterday," he said. "He ran in the front door and out the side door of this place like he knew where he was going." He took a mug-shot photo out of his shirt pocket and handed it to Mora. "Do you know him?" Carr said.

Mora glanced at the photo and handed it back to Carr. "I'm an absentee landlord," he said. "I don't live in Los Angeles. This place is owned by a corporation."

"We figured you might know the guy," Carr interrupted. "His name is Paul LaMonica."

Teddy Mora shook his head. "Never heard of him. Is there anything else?"

"Yeah," Kelly said, examining a hashish pipe on the counter. "How long do you think it'll be before you'll be able to sell dope to the kiddies right along with all the paraphernalia?"

Teddy Mora twirled the car keys. His gaze shifted from Carr to Kelly and back to Carr. "Is that about it? I have things to do around here."

"LaMonica's a fugitive," Carr said. "We're *real* interested in finding him. You've been around long enough to know what I mean. If we can't find him, we'll be back. And that's a promise not a threat."

Ignoring them, Mora turned and spoke casually to his clerk. The agents exited the front door.

Kelly drove along Hollywood Boulevard on the way back downtown. When they stopped at a red light, there were straggly-haired teenage boys on each of the four street corners. One of the young men gave a groin-pump greeting to a passing convertible driven by an older man wearing dark glasses. The man pulled the convertible to the curb and the boy approached.

"Child prostitutes, stores that sell dope fixings . . ." Kelly muttered in a defeated tone. "The whole country is turning to shit. Sometimes I think I'd like to take my wife and kids, chuck everything, and live up in the mountains away from it all. No mind-rotting TV, no forced busing, no dope." He shook his bear-sized head.

"LaMonica comes into town," Carr said, staring at the road ahead. "He stops by the Castaways Lounge and meets with Teddy Mora. They talk business. Linda gets her hooks in and invites him over—"

"For one of her Mata Hari-style interrogations," Kelly interrupted.

"LaMonica makes a telephone call from her place," Carr continued, "and uses the name Bob French. He tells her he plans to leave town the next day." He rubbed his chin. "LaMonica came to L.A. To get something he needed, or maybe to sell a package of bad paper." He had a puzzled expression.

"It could be anything," Kelly said, coming out of his fugue.

"Four-Lima-four from Los Angeles base," blared the Treasury radio. Carr opened the glove compartment, pulled out the microphone, and answered.

"Meet Detective Higgins at the L.A. morgue, third floor."

"Roger," Carr said.

CHAPTER 9

Carr and Kelly stepped into the morgue elevator and waited for the doors to close. There was an odor of formaldehyde. "Hold it!" shouted someone in the hall. Carr pushed the "open door" button. A freckled man in a pale green surgical outfit backed into the lift, pulling a gurney with a sheet covering everything on it except a yellowed toe.

Kelly grimaced and pushed the third-floor button.

"You guys here for a murder autopsy?" said the medic. A surgeon's cap balanced precariously on a mop of curly red hair. His voice had a tone of anticipation.

Kelly shook his head no. He stared at the yellow toe.

"This turkey electrocuted himself," said the red-haired man. "He wrapped an electrical wire around his head, grounded himself in his bathtub, and just put in the old plug. *Zappo!*"

Kelly shook his head sadly. "Poor guy," he said.

The elevator stopped. The doors opened. "He got a real *charge* out of it!" the doc said. He laughed and waited for the agents to join in. When they didn't, he rolled the body out of the elevator and headed the opposite way down a sterile-looking corridor.

"That's why I hate to come here," Kelly said as they walked down the hall. "These people are all creeps. Real honest-to-god one-hundred-percent *creeps.*"

Carr nodded.

Higgins, a fortyish, crew-cut man who was the size of a football lineman, beckoned them into an office. They sat down around a table covered with bloody knives in transparent plastic envelopes and enlarged color photos of death scenes. One photo was a close-up of the belt around Linda Gleason's neck.

"I'm waiting to observe my second autopsy for the day," Higgins said. "Some gang murders that happened last night." He ran a hand through his stubble of blond hair. "I've got a few minutes, so I'll give it to you briefly. Your girl died of strangulation and she had multiple head injuries. The murderer bashed her brains in with a heavy lamp base. He did this after he choked her out with a belt. There were no fingerprints in the apartment except for hers and those of a couple of bartenders from the Castaways Lounge she was balling. I showed LaMonica's photograph to every resident of the apartment house. No one could identify him, including the old lady next door. She wasn't wearing her eyeglasses."

"What about the taxi dispatchers?" Carr said.

"Just getting to that," Higgins said. "The taxi company logs show no fare to Linda Gleason's address all day, which probably means that the cabby who drove LaMonica over there pocketed the fare." Higgins stretched his arms over his head. "So unless you can capture LaMonica and talk him into giving us a confession complete enough so that we can corroborate everything he says, we have no murder case." He turned his palms up.

Carr raised his eyebrows. He shook his head. "I've read all his previous arrest reports. LaMonica doesn't confess when he gets arrested. He always goes to the joint without saying a word."

"Then he'll beat the rap," Higgins said. "It's doubtful we could prove *motive* because we can't prove he knew she was the informant. For *means,* the murder weapons have no fingerprints. Proving *opportunity* is out because no one can place him at the scene of the crime. Getting the district attorney to file murder charges in this case would be about as easy as finding a doctor who'd admit a mistake."

Carr stared at the floor for a minute.

Kelly took a photograph from the array on the table and held it up. It was a five-by-eight of a group of pigeons pecking at what looked like popcorn strewn along a blood-spattered sidewalk. "What the hell is this?" he said with a disgusted look.

"Pigeons eating human guts," said the cop. "Couple of Mexican chaps disemboweled one another on Wabash Avenue day before yesterday. Machetes. A young officer took the photo to prove that he tried to secure the original crime scene like he was supposed to. But the birds showed up for the feast."

Kelly tossed the photo down.

Carr said thanks to the detective. Then the two agents headed out of the office and down the hall toward the elevator.

"Next time we come here I'm going to wait in the car," Kelly said. "I'm getting too old for this shit. I really am."

"Me too," Carr said. He gave his partner a punch on the shoulder.

In the moonlight the water along the coast was inky, its waves gray, ominous.

Paul LaMonica pulled off the El Camino Real highway onto a bumpy road that led to the beach. After a hundred yards or so, his headlights illuminated a stucco building surrounded by sports cars and Cadillacs. The structure was the size of a small tract house. For God only knows what reason, it had been built catty-corner to the water. Like the rest of Baja architecture, it looked unfinished. Like some revolutionary slogan, the word *Teddy's* had been painted in red above the entrance.

LaMonica parked his car and got out. The sound of Mariachi music and drunken conversation mixed with that of the waves slapping against the rocks. He went in.

Inside the dimly lit hangout was a circular bar and a few tables occupied by as many boisterous, garishly dressed women as men—mostly bikers and their broads. Three Mexican guitar players strummed in the corner.

Everyone, including the musicians, had their eyes on LaMonica as he made his way to a table.

Behind the bar, Teddy Mora filled shot glasses from a half-gallon tequila bottle. He wore a Stetson with a red band and feather, and gold necklaces over a T-shirt with a cartoon illustration of a man with an oversized, drooling tongue. He waved at LaMonica and everyone stopped staring. LaMonica sat at an empty table.

A few minutes later Mora moved to LaMonica's table carrying a tequila bottle and two glasses. He set the items on the table and pulled a lemon out of his trouser pocket. Using a penknife, he sliced it into wedges. He looked around to see if anyone was listening.

"I'm running out of twenties," Teddy said, wiping the wet knife on his T-shirt.

LaMonica shook his head. "They're all gone," he said.

Teddy filled the glasses and sprinkled salt on the back of his hand. Taking a lick of the salt, he tossed back a shot of tequila. He chomped on a lemon wedge and spit the rind on the floor. "That's too bad," he said. "Everybody wants 'em." He laughed. "I even tossed a few in with my bar receipts and deposited them in the bank." He laughed again.

"That's what you can do with my newest *thing,*" La Monica said.

Teddy Mora looked puzzled.

"Traveler's checks," LaMonica said. "You can dump a few in with your bar receipts. Even though they're counterfeit, the traveler's-check company will pay off, stand good for them. If they didn't, all of you legit businessmen would refuse to accept them and the company would go out of business."

"In other words, the company is willing to take the loss," Teddy said.

"Exactly."

"Then lay some of that nice paper on me, my good man. Teddy *loves* Paulie's paper." He stuck out his bony hand.

LaMonica pulled an envelope out of his back pocket and handed it to Mora. "You're the only person besides myself who knows about these. You will not deal them to anyone else. Use them yourself or throw them away."

"In other words, Paulie has bigger plans for the checks. Teddy gets the picture. Your secret is safe with Teddy," Mora said reassuringly.

"Has Sandy been around?" LaMonica asked.

"She stops in for a few almost every night," Teddy said. "She's got a new boyfriend. He sticks with her like glue. Do you know who I'm talking about?"

LaMonica shook his head.

"The spook that drives the gold-colored Caddy. I think his name is Cole," Teddy said, "but he calls himself Mr. Cool."

"Never heard of him."

"Typical spook weight-pumper," Mora said. "He just got out of San Quentin. Supposedly he's wanted for violation of parole."

"How tight is she hooked up with this Mr. Spook or whoever he is?" LaMonica said. He drank a shot of tequila and bit into the lemon. Warmth rushed to his face.

"From the looks of it she ain't just 'trying one out,'" Teddy said. "You'll probably have to go through him if you want to use her."

A young man wearing a safari jacket slid in the door and surveyed the crowd. He had greasy ducktailed hair and no color in his face. An Oriental woman in skintight clothing followed him, her T-shirted nipples pointing like camouflaged radar. The man gave a clenched-fist salute to Teddy and the couple sat down at a table with two well-dressed Mexican men.

Teddy Mora shook his head. "Things are nothing like the old days," he said. "That asshole will sit right there at that table and will, without so much as lowering his motherfuckin' voice, settle on a price with those two pushers. Then he'll probably do the deal; yes, *actually make the goddamn transfer,* right out in the parking lot. He'll have his bitch drive the dope across the border tonight. When she gets busted he'll actually wonder *why.* And when she hands him up he'll wonder *why* again. It'll probably never occur to the poor dumb shit that he did everything wrong; that, for all anybody knows, half the customers in this place are federal snitches waiting to tip off the customs people at the border. To that young jack-off, life is what he sees on TV. All the young punks today are out of touch with reality. To them everything is just a game. Maybe it's because they all get probation the first time out these days." Mora leaned into another shot of tequila and bit a lemon wedge. "People have been dropping like flies around here," he said. He wiped his mouth with the back of his hand. "There's gotta be a turkey in the crowd," he whispered, "but I just can't figure out who. Somebody gets arrested almost every day, it seems like. This place is getting a bad name. Couple of American narcs bust in here the other day with the Mexican cops. They handcuffed a guy sitting right at the bar and dragged his ass out of here like a dog—some fugitive from L.A. I mean, like how in the hell did they know he was here?" Teddy's eyes surveyed the other tables suspiciously. "When I figure out who it is, I'll have the cocksucker snuffed out." Teddy chuckled. "Thank God down here it only costs two or three hundred bucks."

"Or just tell me and I'll do the job for free," LaMonica said. He smiled.

Prune-faced Teddy licked the rim of his shot glass. "Remind me never to piss you off, Paulie the Printer," he said.

CHAPTER 10

After an hour or so of driving up and down the streets of Ensenada like a tourist looking for a room, LaMonica found the gold Cadillac with the MR COOL license plate. It was parked in front of a motel that looked like the others in town, a place with lots of rooms built around a swimming pool that was too small and a bar that was larger than the restaurant. He pulled into a lot across the street, where he could keep an eye on the rooms and the car at the same time.

For the next couple of hours he watched the comings and goings of the guests, mostly blue-collar types: hefty men in Bermuda shorts and uninteresting women carrying straw purses. Everyone was in various stages of tanning. They splashed one another in the pool, chased kids, and passed around bags of potato chips.

Leaning back in the seat, LaMonica recalled how he and Sandy Hartzbecker had first met. They'd been sitting on plastic-covered sofas in the dingy reception area of the federal parole office in downtown Los Angeles. His first impression of her was that she was a woman who would be impossible to describe. She was neither homely nor attractive, and her face, as well as her height, weight, bra size, and shape of hips, was totally unremarkable. Even her age would be difficult to guess. She had crow's-feet but it was difficult to tell whether they were caused by excessive exposure to sun and wind or the normal aging process. She wore a loose-fitting blouse and jeans, and cheap tennis shoes. Her mousy-brown hair was in pigtails, and her complexion was forgettable; unblemished and devoid of makeup of any kind.

She was precisely the type of woman he had been looking for.

He could tell by the form letter she kept folding and unfolding that it was probably her first post-release visit.

"Who's your parole officer?" he said.

She referred to the form. "Mr. Askew."

"He's mine, too," LaMonica said. He lowered his voice. "He's big on playing big brother—a God-squad type. Cry on his shoulder a little bit and ask for advice on something. He'll love it. If you ask, he'll go for waiving the monthly visits."

"Thanks for the information." Her German accent was muted and and as dreary as her appearance.

After his visit to the parole officer, LaMonica waited in the hallway outside the office. When she came out, they entered the elevator together. The door closed.

"You were right," she said. "He went for it."

"Where'd you do your time?" he said.

"Terminal Island."

The elevator door opened. They dodged through a crowded lobby onto the street. LaMonica offered her a ride and she accepted.

"What are you into?" she said when they were in the car.

"Paper." LaMonica started the engine and slipped into the halting downtown traffic.

"I did some once," she said. "Hundreds. I passed them in clothing stores in the San Fernando Valley." She gave an amused smile. "I bought so many cheap blouses I could have opened my own shop."

"What's your business?"

"My old man's business was heroin. I did time because I

carried for him. I saw the feds following me so I got scared and threw the bundles out the window. It was the stupidest thing I've ever done in my whole life. I just lost my cool. When they arrested me they told me that if I hadn't thrown the stuff, they never would have known I was carrying. Every time I think about it it makes me sick."

"Who's your old man?"

"He's dead," she said. "A rip-off. It happened while I was in." She sighed. "But it may have been for the best. If I was with him now I'd probably be right back in all the shit."

LaMonica pulled up to a run-down apartment house in the shadow of the Ambassador Hotel. Without asking, he turned off the engine and accompanied her up some steps to her door. She unlocked it and he followed her in. The one-bedroom apartment was sparsely furnished: a worn sofa and chair, a stack of German-language paperbacks on an end table next to a framed photograph of Sandy holding hands with a black man and dressed in army fatigues. They were posed on a cobblestone street.

"That was my old man, in case you're wondering," she said without emotion. She tossed her purse down and sauntered into the tiny kitchen. She opened a cabinet and pulled out a bottle of bourbon. "He was a dope fiend and pusher, but he was always good to me."

"I guess that's what it's all about," LaMonica said in his most sincere tone.

They spent the rest of the afternoon sharing the quart of bourbon. Red-cheeked and tipsy from the liquor, she recounted her life story: a small town outside Munich, a taxidriver father whose goal in life was to sell enough blackmarket G.I. liquor to buy his own *Gasthaus*, a mother who ran away with the town butcher and later came back, a Roman Catholic school whose nuns administered swats at the drop of a hat, and finally the story of her sister. Sandy Hartzbecker told the tale as if she were recounting the success story of the century: "She tricked in a fancy whorehouse in Stuttgart for three years and saved her money. When she left, she had enough to buy a Mercedes-Benz and a new identity. She moved to Frankfurt and started life all over again; told everyone she was a widow, that her husband had been a doctor who lost his life in a car accident. She ended up marrying a rich lawyer. It proved to me that people can make something of themselves if they really want to. I knew that I could be more than a waitress in a G.I. bar for the rest of my life. I left Germany and came to the U.S. with my old man."

That evening after some sex talk he followed her into the bedroom. As they undressed he noticed her sinewy housemaid's shoulders, her proud, dark nipples. She threw back the covers and climbed on the bed. He joined her and discovered that her sexual abilities were pretty much along the lines of her general appearance: mediocre at best. Afterward, they lay in the prespiration-soaked bed. She lit a cigarette.

"You're different than other men," she said.

"Howzat?"

"Because you're gentle," she said. "I loved the way you went for my tits. You took your time with me and didn't rush. A tit man is a gentle man. I hate to be just *used*."

The next year of nights was a blur of hotels and motels from Las Vegas to Newport Beach, the days spent passing and selling counterfeit money. Passing one bill at a time at shopping centers and department stores, fast-food joints, grocery markets. LaMonica would wait in the car as Sandy Hartzbecker went from store to store getting change for a twenty or fifty. With package deals, he would make the arrangements with a buyer and she would deliver the bills to a phone booth or a rental locker or a hotel room and pick up the payment. All in all, it was just like the song: *a really good year* . . . until Sandy's arrest.

A black man with an Afro that looked half a foot high came out of a room on the second floor. He glanced around suspiciously and walked down the stairs to the gold Cadillac. He got in the car and drove off.

LaMonica locked his sedan and trotted up the stairs two at a time. He tried the door handle. It was unlocked. He pushed the door open. There was the smell of sex in the room.

Sandy Hartzbecker got up off the bed. She was naked, but made no attempt to cover herself. "What the hell do you want?" she asked.

"Just to talk," LaMonica said.

She grabbed a pair of Levi's off the end of the bed and wiggled into them. "The answer is no," she said. Having yanked on a pullover, she strode to the dresser mirror. Angrily, she picked up a brush. Ignoring his presence, she yanked it through her hair.

"Can we just have a drink? For old times' sake, shall we say?"

She tossed the brush down and faced him. "The only 'old times' I remember was when I took chances for you and ended up going to the fuckin' joint. You better get out of here before my boyfriend gets back. He can press three hundred pounds."

"Your cut in this new thing would be twenty-five G's. I can prove it to you on paper."

"You are not part of my life anymore," she said. "I'm not into being a mule or a slave for any man. I'm tired of being *used*. I'm looking out for myself. You knew I was down here and you never so much as looked me up to say hello. Now you need me for a *thing* and you want to buy me a drink."

"I tried to bail you out."

"And I'm sure you tried to send me flowers, too," she said. "There's no need for bullshit. We did our thing and now it's over. I don't need you anymore. I do enough coke and smack deals to keep me in clothes and motels. I'm not greedy. I put everything together myself. No moneymen, no partners, no getting busted for somebody else. I'm my own person, and that's the way I like it. I don't want to work for you or anybody else. I did a lot of thinking when I was in Terminal Island. I look at life a lot more realistically now. I'm no longer your average dumb farm girl."

"As a matter of fact, you're the most intelligent woman I've ever met," LaMonica said. His gaze was dead serious.

"Yeah, well my brains didn't keep me from getting busted for you and going to the joint."

"All I ask is one drink. If you want to talk I'll be down in the bar." He walked out the door and closed it behind him.

The bar was a spacious, well-lit place with wicker chairs and decorative tiles on the walls and floors. Paul LaMonica sat at a table and sipped a drink. He kept looking out the window toward Sandy's room. Except for a couple of fishermen at the bar exchanging jokes with the bartender, he was alone in the place.

Twenty minutes later Sandy strutted in and LaMonica took a deep breath. The fishermen elbowed one another as she shouted, "Cuba libre, no ice," to the bartender and sat down at LaMonica's table. "I don't like people sneaking up on me," she said.

"Neither do I."

Sandy Hartzbecker dug a filter tip out of her purse and flamed it with a gold lighter. She sucked smoke. "So many people have gotten busted down here in the last few weeks that I've become paranoid," she said. "And I'm not talking about getting taken down behind a few spoons of coke or a brick of weed. I'm talking about the other night when the *federales* stormed into Teddy's and dragged some dude right out the door. They drove him straight to the border and shoved him across the white line to a carload of FBI agents. He was good for some bank jobs in San Francisco. But how did they know he was sitting there in Teddy's? It's scary. Really fuckin' scary." The bartender set a drink down in front of her and walked away. She poked the ice with her finger.

"The simple explanation," LaMonica said, "is that someone who hangs around Teddy's is a snitch."

"There was a time when it seemed like you could trust everyone there," Sandy said. She used the straw.

"Trust everyone at Teddy's?" LaMonica laughed.

Her face reddened. She pointed a finger at his face. "Look, you sonofabitch, I don't have to take any shit from you. The last time we did something together I'm the one who ended up holding the bag, and to this day I'm not even sure what happened. You told me that the pit boss was *wired*. 'Just drop the phony fifties on the pass line,' you said. And without so much as asking you a question, I did just that. He was *wired* all right! The next thing I know the whole Las Vegas Police Department is dragging me away. Did you know that out of the corner of my eye I saw you sneaking off toward the slot machines? The feds offered to let me go if I would tell them who gave me the counterfeit money. But I kept my mouth shut. I protected you. And did I ask you for any help when they sent me to the penitentiary? No. I escaped on my own, without one bit of help from anyone. And I'll tell you this, I'm a much stronger person for the experience." She took a deep drag on her cigarette.

"I've never forgotten that you stood up for me, that you didn't hand me up to the feds," LaMonica said. "You might say that I want to make it up to you with this new caper."

"Bullshit," she said. Tears welled in her eyes. It occurred to LaMonica that he had never seen her cry.

"I know a lot of women who would love to take a shot at twenty-five grand," LaMonica said.

"Hundreds of women would jump at a chance to make twenty-five bucks, much less twenty-five grand. But you and I know that's not the goddamn point. You want me because you know I won't snitch on you if I get caught. You know I've stood the test of fire."

"In certain ways that's true."

"You are the most selfish person I have ever known," Sandy said. "Everything revolves around *you*. It's what turned me off about you. I can't believe we spent almost a year together." She shook her head.

"In this new thing you wouldn't even have to cross the border," LaMonica said.

The bartender brought another drink. He set it down.

"The answer is still no."

LaMonica was silent for a moment. He reached into his

back pocket and pulled out the counterfeit passport. He opened it and showed Sandy her photograph. Her eyes lit up. He shoved it back in his pocket.

"The passport would be your bonus," he said.

Sandy Hartzbecker looked out the window for a while. "You actually *like* to fuck with a person's mind, don't you? You know I want to go back home. I'd be safe. The Germans would never extradite one of their own citizens."

"A few simple meetings on this side of the border is all I'm asking," he said.

"Meetings with who?"

"With a turkey, a square who won't know who you are. You will play a part. You'll be in on the whole thing with me, so you'll be able to see exactly how much money is involved. I intend to split fifty-fifty with you, and you'll be right in the middle with me to see that there's no back-stabbing, no rip-offs. We would be partners."

The fishermen laughed hysterically about something and ordered more tequila.

Sandy Hartzbecker sipped her drink and set the glass down. She lit a cigarette and puffed twice. Smoke floated from her mouth. "Will you repeat what you've promised me in front of my boyfriend?" Her lips were pursed in a determined manner.

"Sure," LaMonica said sarcastically, "and then maybe we should drive down to Teddy's and announce our business to every American thief and dope pusher in Baja. Let's let the whole world in on it. *What the hell.*"

"You don't have to tell him what it's about, and I won't either. I swear. But I want you to make the commitment in front of him." She lowered her voice. "If I don't get my cut when it's over, then he'll come for you. He'll be my insurance."

"Maybe we should get a lawyer to draw up a contract?" LaMonica said with a sneer. "Can your nigger read?"

"You are a bigoted chauvinist pig," she said, her voice cracking. "Mr. Cool is more of a together person than *you* ever could be. It was a *black* man not a *white* man who married me and brought me to the U.S. I would still be serving beer to G.I.s for four marks an hour if it hadn't been for him. He was a dope fiend, but he treated me better than any white man ever has—*including you.*"

LaMonica stood up. "I'll be at Teddy's tonight," he said. "If you want in, meet me there. You can bring your boyfriend." He walked out the door wondering whether he should have played it a little softer.

CHAPTER 11

LaMonica had been in Teddy's for over an hour, sitting at a corner table sipping beer. Teddy flitted from table to table with his tequila bottle and lemon. Sandy came in the door followed by her boyfriend. Mr. Cool wore a form-fitting T-shirt the same color as his skin. His biceps were puffed, veiny. Sandy pointed and he strolled to LaMonica's table. Unsmiling, the black man sat down. He had boozy, red-rimmed eyes and a moon-shaped scar on his cheek. Looking self-conscious, Sandy walked past them to the bar.

LaMonica stared at the weightlifter with a blank expression. "I'm offering Sandy a piece of a thing I have under way. Her part will be a few simple meetings. I'm promising her twenty-five grand when it's over." He sipped his drink.

The black man made a half smile. "Is this a paper thing?"

"I guess you could say that," LaMonica said.

"Just what kind of paper do we be talking about?" Mr. Cool folded his arms and leaned forward on the cocktail table. The table tilted.

LaMonica sat back as if the man across from him were diseased. "High-quality paper."

"Then we be talking about funny money," Mr. Cool said. "Is that what we be talking about?"

LaMonica sipped his drink, then wiped his mouth with the back of his hand. "What part don't you understand, brother?"

"Just exactly what the fuck do the lady have to *do,* man?" Mr. Cool said. "Some things people have to do are worth more money than other things people have to do."

"If the lady decides she wants in, then she will do exactly what the fuck I *tell* her to do," LaMonica said. "That's what she has to do."

"You didn't answer the muthafuckin' question."

"Why don't you give it to me again?"

"Man, why don't you quit the shuckin' and jivin' and get down to talkin' some business? The lady asked me to check things out and make sure it all goes right for her, that she ain't going to get ripped off. If I don't give her the go-ahead, then she for damn sure ain't gonna join your little party. Do you see where I'm comin' from?"

"Like I said, her part will be a couple of meetings with a sucker," LaMonica said. "She plays a part. We score and split fifty thousand. This is a guarantee."

"In other words, the lady have to show her face. And if she have to be showing her face, then she's right out there on Front Street when the pigs come around with their pictures," he said. He lit a menthol cigarette.

LaMonica looked the man in the eye. He said nothing.

"You'll have to deal with me if she don't get what's comin' to her," the black man said.

"She'll get it," LaMonica said. "But it won't be because I'm afraid of you, nigger."

Mr. Cool stared at LaMonica for a moment. Then he got up and went to the bar. He and Sandy whispered. Sandy came back to the table and said, "Okay, when and where?" There were tears in her eyes.

"I'll pick you up at your motel day after tomorrow," LaMonica said. "Pack a bag."

"Where are we going?"

"Up to Tijuana."

During the twenty-minute ride from the airport the cab driver drawled on about how much Houston had grown and LaMonica acted as if he were interested. He pulled up in front of a gunmetal-gray building with letters over a bank of glass doors that spelled "National Headquarters Travelers Chex Incorporated." LaMonica paid the taxi fare, including tip, and stepped out onto the sidewalk. He checked every pocket in his clothing as a final security measure, making sure he carried no identification with his real name. He strode into the building.

The reception area was decorated with a Texas state flag, travel photos, and a blowup of a purplish traveler's check. The receptionist, a young Mexican woman with dark lips and eyes, was courteous. He told her he wanted to talk to the director of security. She made a brief phone call and showed him into an office decorated with police paraphernalia: insignia patches, inscribed billy clubs.

The fat man behind the desk stood up and shook hands. It was hard to tell his age. He had smooth pink cheeks that probably didn't require more than a once-a-week shave. His hair was black and looked as if it had been pasted onto his head in little greasy gobs. He wore a clip-on necktie. "Omar T. Lockhart," he boomed. "I'm the director of security."

LaMonica introduced himself as Roger Brown and handed the man a business card. Lockhart motioned him to a chair. He read the business card out loud: "International Investigative Service."

"Most of my clients are corporations," LaMonica said.

"I see. And what can I do for you?" Lockhart made a little pointless laugh.

"I am a private investigator," LaMonica said. "I represent a client who wants to provide information concerning the counterfeiting of your company's traveler's checks. My client demands anonymity, and I have given her my personal and professional assurances that her identity will be protected. Frankly, she fears for her life."

Omar T. Lockhart slid forward in his chair. He took off his glasses and held them up to the light. "In other words, she wants to be paid a reward for her information," he said, putting the glasses back on. He flexed his eyebrows a few times and coughed without putting a hand over his mouth. "And just how will *you* be paid?"

LaMonica gave a puzzled look. *"My* fee?" he said.

"Yes," Lockhart said, "that is what I'm asking you."

"I'm working on a percentage of the recovery fee plus expenses. That should be no secret."

Lockhart nodded knowingly. He looked out the window.

"I'll get to the point," LaMonica said. "My client has knowledge of a stash of one million dollars in traveler's checks. They're five-hundred-dollar denomination checks."

Lockhart turned to LaMonica. "Do you have a sample?"

LaMonica pulled a business-sized envelope out of his coat pocket and handed it to Lockhart. Lockhart removed the check from the envelope and examined it carefully before putting it back in the envelope.

"And just what do we have to do to get our hands on these checks?" Lockhart said.

"I'll have to convince my client that it's worth the risk."

Lockhart nodded. "I understand."

"She is a very street-wise lady," LaMonica said. "She knows full well that traveler's-check companies bear the full dollar loss on counterfeit checks that are passed. She wants ten percent of the dollar amount of the recovery."

Lockhart laughed. "Just a hundred thousand dollars?" he said. "No way we are going to pay any such reward, my good man. No way."

"I'm just relaying what she's told me. I'm only a middleman." LaMonica stood up and stretched. He went to the window. The view was of a sprawling business area mixing into suburbs; a town of fast-buck artists, chance takers, oil thieves. "I know you'll want to discuss this with your superiors," he said. "Perhaps we could meet again tomorrow?"

Lockhart looked puzzled. He nodded.

"If you do decide to deal with my client, I would insist that you make no contact with the police or FBI until the investigation is in its final stages," LaMonica said. "Police agencies have a tendency to move too quickly and could compromise my client."

"Of course those decisions are ours alone to make," Lockhart said.

LaMonica turned to the security man. "Speaking as a professional private investigator, I'm telling you that my client will not work with the police. Period. I don't intend to waste my time and have the case blown before we are able to locate and recover the counterfeit checks—all of them. There will be plenty of time for the police to make arrests once the investigation is at the proper stage."

"That sounds fair enough," Lockhart said.

The men shook hands and Paul LaMonica walked out the door. Lockhart returned to his desk. After staring at Brown's business card for a few seconds, he dialed the Los Angeles telephone number on it.

A woman answered. "International Investigative Service."

"Mr. Roger Brown, please," he said.

"I'm sorry. Mr. Brown is out of town for a few days. May I tell him who called?"

"I'd prefer to just give him a call in a few days. I have some work for him. Uh, I take it your firm does handle corporate work?"

"Yes," the woman said. "This firm handles private investigations and industrial security work for major corporations. May I take your name and address?"

Lockhart set the receiver down.

The conference room was decorated with a set of Texas longhorns and a color photograph of John Wayne standing in front of the Alamo. He was holding up a book of traveler's checks.

Omar T. Lockhart sat in a seat at the end of the mahogany table next to the vice-president for personnel. The table was filled with men wearing dark suits. He had stood up and given his briefing, using as much police jargon as possible. By the time the questions started, there was a definite air of urgency in the room and Lockhart knew full well that he had created it.

"Who *is* this 'private eye'?" said the gray-haired man at the opposite end of the table. His expression was grim, perhaps a requirement for a chairman of the board.

"I've checked him out, Mr. Stallworth. He's an independent from Los Angeles. He does corporate work mostly."

The eyes at the table went from one man to another like a crowd at a tennis match.

"Just how *good* are these counterfeit checks?" Stallworth said.

"Excellent quality," Lockhart said. He removed a check from a folder and held it up. "Easy to pass," he added, realizing that his usual board-room butterflies had almost gone away. Everyone was looking at the check.

Stallworth spoke. "How many of these have actually been passed?"

"Just a few in Ensenada, Mexico, a couple of days ago. They were passed in a bar," Lockhart said. "They've just started to pop up. For once we're right on top of the operation. We have a chance of recovering the checks before they get into heavy circulation."

"Get him down to some reasonable figure," Stallworth said. "We'll pay, but we're not going to pay full fare."

"And the police?" Lockhart said.

"The private investigator is probably right in that regard," Stallworth said. "If we bring in the police or the FBI at this point, they will take control. Naturally, they'll be more interested in arresting crooks than recovering the counterfeit checks before we end up eating a million-dollar loss. For the time being let's keep the police out of it."

Stallworth looked at his watch. "I want you to report to me every day on this matter."

"Yes, sir," Lockhart said.

Stallworth pushed his chair back. Everyone stood up. The chairman of the board left the room.

Omar T. Lockhart felt perspiration trickle down the middle of his back.

CHAPTER 12

Carr and Kelly sat in a sedan across the street from the Castaways Lounge. The tavern was sandwiched between a porno shop with a cloth hanging over its front door and a storefront telephone answering service that Carr knew was used as a contact point for whores and pimps. Over the front entrance to the bar was a sign that read "No T-shirts or Bare Feet."

As usual, Kelly insisted on getting out of the sedan and stretching his legs every half hour. So far he had done this four or five times.

He finished reading a newspaper and tossed it in the backseat. "Have you ever thought about what this does to a person's health?" Kelly said.

Carr gave him a puzzled look.

"Just sitting on your butt all day in the front seat of a car," Kelly said. "Lack of exercise, food can't digest properly. It's bad for the circulation, too. Just as soon as we get off work, what do we do? We sit on our butts at Ling's bar, swilling drinks and eating greasy chicken rolls. There's absolutely nothing healthful about the job. If you let it, the job will kill ya, outright kill ya. Death by blood clots in the legs."

"Linda said he comes here every Friday without fail," Carr said, gazing across the street.

"We'll probably still be sitting here at midnight," Kelly said.

Carr shrugged.

Less than half an hour later, a Cadillac pulled up in front of the bar. Teddy Mora opened the door, got out, and glanced around. He was wearing a tropical shirt, white pants, and sandals.

The T-men ducked down in the seat as Mora sauntered through the front door. They sat up again.

"Okay," Kelly said. "The asshole showed up. If he's peddling counterfeit money, he's got to have some on him. I say we stroll right into the place, throw him up against a wall, and see what he's got in his goddamn pockets. Nothing to lose, really, and we might even get lucky."

"Let's wait until we catch his act," Carr said.

"We could be here forever," Kelly said.

Three hours later, Mora exited the front door and looked around. He walked to the Cadillac and got in.

"Let's just grab him and see if he's holding," Kelly said.

"Not yet," Carr said. His eyes were riveted to the Cadillac.

Mora started the Caddy and drove past them. Carr fumbled with the ignition and squealed tires making a U-turn. He followed, letting Mora stay a block or so ahead. Suddenly the Cadillac pulled into a small parking lot next to a hamburger stand. Mora parked and got out. He shuffled into a telephone booth and closed the door. Moments later he exited the booth and returned to his vehicle. He started the engine and drove off.

"Pretty short phone call," Carr said, his eyes still on the phone booth.

"You're right, partner." Kelly got out of the car, strolled to the phone booth, and stepped inside. A minute later he returned to the sedan and climbed in. "The booth is loaded. There's a stack of bogus twenties taped under the phone box," Kelly said, digging around in the glove compartment. He found a set of handcuffs and stuffed them in his pocket.

In less than ten minutes, a white Porsche with a bumper sticker that read "Happiness is Being Single" pulled up next to the hamburger stand. An emaciated-looking young man wearing tight Levi's and a tank top got out on the driver's side. He had a grayish complexion. Tugging nervously at his mop of curly hair, he surveyed the street carefully. Finally, he stepped into the telephone booth and pushed the accordion door closed.

"He was in the Castaways earlier," Kelly said. "I remember the car."

The young man picked up the telephone receiver and held it to his ear. His other hand sought the bottom of the phone box. He shoved something into his pants pocket and opened the door. After glancing around, he stepped out of the booth and headed for the Porsche.

"He's got it!" Carr said on his way out of the sedan. He ran across the street at full speed. As he approached, the young man ripped an envelope from his pocket and tossed it on the ground. He dove for the door of the sports car. Carr grabbed the man's arm and spun it behind him. "Federal officers," he said. "You're under arrest." The young man gave a moan. Kelly snatched the envelope off the ground. He handed Carr the handcuffs. Carr fastened them onto the man's wrists. He dragged the struggling man across the street to the sedan and shoved him into the backseat.

Kelly climbed in next to the prisoner. He thumbed through the stack of counterfeit notes as Carr walked around the sedan and got into the driver's seat.

The young man's eyes were shut. "I'm fucked," he said, shaking his head. "I'm on parole right now. I'll get violated. *God damn it!*" There were inch-long strands of curly hair growing on the man's sallow cheeks. His nose was running.

Kelly handed Carr the packet of counterfeit money. The T-man looked at it without expression for a moment. The prisoner squirmed. "Pretty rough," Carr said. "Taking a trip back to the joint for such a little package . . ."

The young man's mouth hung open like a baby bird's. His eyes were shut. "God damn it," he cried. "I shoulda never left my apartment. I had nightmares last night. Shit comes down on me whenever I have nightmares. My roommate told me not to do anything today . . . *God damn it.*"

"We want Teddy Mora," Carr said without emotion.

The man was silent for what must have been a full minute. "I ain't no snitch," he said.

"I didn't say you were," Carr responded. "But you just *might* be a businessman. If you are a businessman, you'll realize that now is the time to make a deal."

"Exactly what kind of a deal?" The man leaned forward in the seat.

"You for Teddy Mora," Carr said.

The young man looked out the window for a while and sniffled a few times. "I'll never testify. I'm not crazy. I've seen what happens to people when they—"

"You won't have to testify," Carr interrupted. He lit a cigarette.

"If I take this thing to trial I might beat it altogether. I beat my first case that way. My lawyer told me what to say." He twisted around to wipe his nose on his shoulder. He missed. "The assistant U.S. attorney was a broad with wire hair. She kept trying to use big words; got all screwed up when she asked questions. My lawyer told me he met her at a lawyer's party after the trial. She cried about losing the case. He said she blew him in the front seat of his Mercedes after the party. He tells everybody the story."

"On the other hand, you might go to trial and lose," Carr said.

"That's what happened the second time," the young man said. "The judge sentenced me to probation on the case."

"There's a chance you might get a little prison time for the third offense," Carr said.

The man nodded. "Just happened to a friend of mine. He got six months—that means two months in the joint minus good time and all." He shook his head sadly.

"On the other hand, why do even two months?" Carr said.

The man sat quietly for a few minutes. He leaned his head down to wipe his nose on a knee. He missed.

"Exactly what would I have to do?"

"Just phone Teddy and tell him you want some more," Carr said.

"Then will you let me go?"

"Yes."

The young man furrowed his brow. His head turned from Carr to Kelly and back to Carr. "I want it in writing," he said. "I don't trust cops. I've been screwed before."

"We don't put things in writing," Carr said.

The prisoner leaned forward and attempted to wipe his dripping nose on his knee. Again he missed. He closed his mouth and inhaled.

"This guy is making me sick," Kelly said. "Let's book him."

"If you won't put it in writing, will you repeat what you've just said in front of my lawyer?"

"We hate lawyers," Carr told him.

Nothing was said for a few minutes.

"Will you let me go as soon as I make the call?" the young man said.

"As soon as you make the call," Carr said.

The man leaned back in the seat. He was silent again. Finally, he spoke. "He'll know it was me."

Carr stuffed the counterfeit money back in its envelope. He initialed and dated it, then pulled a rubber band off the rearview mirror and wrapped it around the envelope. Roughly he shoved the packet into his inside coat pocket.

102

"You're right," Carr said. He started the engine.

The young man sat up. "Where are we going?"

"To lock you up," Carr said. He put the car in gear.

"Okay. I'll call him," the young man said. "But I've never snitched before. I really haven't."

Carr turned off the engine. Kelly reached behind the man's back and unlocked the handcuffs. He opened the car door and ushered the prisoner to the telephone booth. Carr followed. Kelly dropped a dime in the slot and handed the prisoner the receiver. He dialed, with Kelly looming over him like a grizzly.

He asked to speak with Teddy Mora. A few seconds went by. "It's me," he said. "I picked up the . . . uh . . . letter at the phone company. Yes, everything is okay." He bit his lip. "It's just that the letter isn't big enough. I need another one of the same size. I wasn't thinking when I placed my first order. I'm planning to take a trip and the letter won't last. I want to have enough to last throughout the trip." The young man's face contorted. He bit harder on his lip. "Well, then you can just forget it, man. Like I can score somewhere else. If you don't want to go to the trouble of delivering another letter, I'll just take my business elsewheres . . . okay, man . . . okay . . . The same place. You know I'm good for it . . . I don't like to talk on the phone either. Right on." The young man hung up the phone. "He's coming to deliver another package to this phone booth," he said. "He was pissed off that I didn't order a bigger one to start with. I did what you wanted." He shook his head sadly. "Now I know what it feels like to rat on somebody." He wiped his nose with two fingers and rubbed the fingers on his trousers. "I shouldn't have done it," he said.

Carr's thumb pointed to the Porsche. "Nice to meet you," he said.

"I wasn't sure you were going to keep your word," the man said.

Carr mocked a smile. The man trotted to the Porsche,

climbed in, and drove off. Carr and Kelly returned to the government sedan.

Teddy Mora arrived less than ten minutes later. He parked his Cadillac next to the phone booth and got out.

The Treasury men had their hands on the door handles. They vaulted out of the sedan and broke into a run. They hit Mora like the Rams' line, knocking him to the ground. They each grabbed an arm and pressed him to the pavement. Carr's fingers flew to the man's pockets and pulled out a stack of twenties.

"I was set up," Mora said as Kelly snapped handcuffs onto his wrists.

CHAPTER 13

The Field Office interview room was paneled with cheap acoustical fiberboard and was, as all police interview rooms are, less than adequate in size. Carr, with Kelly at his side filling out an arrest report, stared at Mora across a small table. He asked him about LaMonica.

Mora's arms were folded across his chest. "I saw LaMonica a couple of days ago in the Castaways," he said. "I see a lot of people there."

"What did you talk about?" Carr said.

"About money. We always talk about money—business deals. I'm an entrepreneur."

"Where do you know him from?" Carr said.

Mora unfolded his arms and tried to rest them in his lap. This didn't work. He folded them across his chest again. "Terminal Island. We did time together. I'm sure you already know that."

"So you talked about money . . ." Carr said.

"That's right. He had some kind of a deal going, and it turned to shit. Some kind of a real-estate deal. Of course he didn't go into detail about it. I assumed it had turned to shit when he came and asked me for a loan. I told him no. That's all I know about him. As far as my head shop, he was there once and he probably figured it was a good place to escape through . . . the alley and all."

Carr stood up and removed his coat. He hung it on the back of his chair. He sat down again. "Where can we find him?" he said.

"I have no idea. Maybe San Francisco or Las Vegas. But I truthfully have no idea where he lives," Mora said.

Carr was silent for a moment. He looked at Kelly. "If you don't tell us everything you know about LaMonica, we'll be forced to camp out on your ass just like we did today. We'll either end up arresting you again or putting you out of business, or both."

"Get the picture, clown?" Kelly said.

Mora stared at the wall. Sitting there, his sagging body barely fitting the government-issue chair, the angular man looked foolish, perhaps inconsequential. "LaMonica lives out of the state," he said. "I swear I don't know where. He was here in L.A. putting together some sort of a legitimate business deal. If you know anything at all about him, you'll know that he never tells anyone his business. As God is my witness, that's all I know about the sonofabitch. Now will you let me post bail? I have appointments to keep."

Carr stood up and opened the door. He nodded at Kelly.

Kelly stood up. "Sure," he said. "We wouldn't want to keep all those nice folks down at the Castaways waiting for their twenties." He grabbed the man's arm and pulled him out the door.

Carr and Kelly pulled up in front of a large store front with a sign that read "Lithographic Supply Service of Los Angeles." They went in.

Three hours later they were still there, coats off, crowded around a messy desk in the manager's office. The manager, a neat, older man who wore glasses with wire frames and a long-sleeved dress shirt that was a size too big, hovered over them as they sorted through piles of invoices.

"How do you know he ordered the supplies from here?" the manager asked sternly.

"Your telephone number was on the toll record we subpoenaed from the phone company," Carr said without looking up.

"And the name *Robert French?*" The manager folded his arms across his chest.

"Someone heard him make a call and order some ink," Carr said. He pushed aside a stack of invoices and dug into another.

"It seems to me," said the manager, "that what we're talking about here is *counterfeiting.*" His tone was grave.

Kelly gave the man an odd look.

"All printers have tried it once," the stern man said.

"What's that?" Carr said. He smiled courteously.

"Counterfeiting," the manager said. "Every printer tries it once. They try it just as a lark and destroy the bills afterward. You know, just to see if they can do it."

"Hot damn!" Kelly said, holding up one of the invoices like a rat's tail. He dropped it in front of Carr.

Carr read the invoice. It listed a sale of black, blue, green, and red ink plus fifteen reams of No. 53 paper to Robert French. Carr handed the invoice to the manager.

The manager studied the paper with a determined look. "Fifty-three is Ardmore Bond, a fairly high-quality paper. We don't get much call for it. This was a cash deal. An over-the-counter transaction."

Carr scribbled something in his notebook and stuffed it into his coat pocket. The agents stood up to leave and Carr thanked the manager.

"No thanks are necessary," he said with a sour look. "This shop has been broken into twice during the last year. I hope you catch the man you're looking for and put him in a penitentiary *forever.* I mean that from the bottom of my heart. *Forever.*" He pursed his lips.

"We'll sure try," Carr said on his way out the door. Kelly gave the man a little salute.

Carr and Kelly were alone in the squad room.

Files, all bearing LaMonica's name, were spread out across Carr's desk. Most of them were marked "Career Criminal," as if such a term had real meaning. Carr had spent the last two hours carefully going over the reports, summaries, and evaluations in them. The Treasury main file included specimen photographs of the counterfeit notes LaMonica had printed throughout the years, mixed in with arrest sheets, conviction forms, intelligence reports, and a stack of booking photographs in which LaMonica's hair became progressively grayer, his jowls slacker. He and Carr were about the same age.

The only remarkable difference from other such files was the absence of confession forms. Even LaMonica's first arrest (caught red-handed in a bank changing twenties into hundreds) reflected a refusal to give out anything other than his name. As a matter of fact, after his last arrest, he had refused even that.

Carr pulled a memorandum from a banded stack of papers covered by a note labeled: "Not for Dissemination Outside Department of Justice." It read:

TO: Chief Federal Probation Officer
FROM: Carl Teagarten—Deputy Federal Probation Officer
Subject: Probationer Paul A. LaMonica—Six-Week Release Report

1. Although probationer LaMonica has a bad habit of falling back into a criminal pattern, he has been out of federal prison for six weeks now and seems to be adjusting. Although he has not gained employment yet, he tells me that he has made a number of applications seeking work as a salesman. I have not allowed him to seek any printing-related occupation for the obvious reasons.

2. LaMonica remains somewhat of a loner and tells me that his free time is spent reading and going to the movies.

3. He rented a fairly expensive apartment in Beverly Hills last week. When I questioned him about it he was very cooperative. Apparently he has recently come into some sort of an inheritance from a distant relative (I haven't had time to verify this, but hope to by the next six-week report). He also made a down payment on a sports car with the same source of income.

4. I have received a number of calls from various law-enforcement agencies for LaMonica's current address, but have refused to provide it under terms of the Privacy Act.

5. Overall, Mr. LaMonica seems to be adjusting quite well at present. He continues to have an overwhelming desire to be accepted by others.

Carr shook his head. He turned to Kelly who was dialing a phone at the next desk. "Ever meet anyone who didn't have a desire to be accepted?"

"Whatsat?" Kelly said.

"Never mind," Carr said. He read the last report in the file. It was a year old and described how LaMonica had been caught in his Beverly Hills apartment with $50,000 in counterfeit twenties.

Carr closed the file.

Kelly jammed the phone down. "That was headquarters," he said. "LaMonica learned to print years ago in the Terminal Island print shop—some sort of a prison *rehabilitation* program." He gave a harsh laugh.

Carr stood up and stretched. He walked to the window. "LaMonica is getting ready to print," he said. "He bought black, green, red, and blue ink and a lot of paper. He would need black and green in order to print money, but I can't figure the blue and red."

Kelly shrugged. "Who the hell knows?" he said. "But there's one thing you can count on. He wouldn't buy ink and paper unless he already had everything else he needed: press, platemaker, photo equipment. He's probably running off a load somewhere right now."

"There's another thing that's for sure," Carr said, still staring out the window. "We don't have any leads."

Chapter 14

It was Saturday afternoon.

Charles Carr slowed down to the speed limit as he approached the garish neon billboards that marked the beginning of the Las Vegas strip. He'd been lounging around Sally's apartment drinking coffee that morning when Sally had pointed at a newspaper advertisement for Las Vegas. With that, she'd jumped up and started throwing things into an overnight bag. "If you won't go with me, I'll go alone," she said.

He went with her. And during the trip she managed to talk the whole way. It was as if she were trying to compensate Carr for the long hours of sagebrush and telephone-line scenery. Her topics were familiar ones: Judge Malcolm's college-age girl friend, the stenographers association's proposed fifteen-day bus tour of Europe, burgeoning rent and inflation, her sister's beautiful and talented children, and Judge Malcolm's shrewish, menopausal wife.

Sally finally stopped talking. She slid over next to him and rested her head on his shoulder. "It's been such a long time since we've taken one of our spur-of-the-moment trips," she said. "Get an idea and just *go*." She slid a hand inside his shirt and touched the hair on his chest. "You're so quiet."

At the check-in desk of the Silver Dollar Hotel and Casino, a mirrored place with a casino lobby the size of a football field, Carr signed the guest register "Mr. and Mrs. Charles Carr."

They spent the evening strolling in and out of the casinos, sipping cocktails, playing slot machines, people-watching along the strip. Carr rolled dice for a while at one place, but stopped when he realized Sally was bored. They caught the midnight stage show at the Dunes Hotel and afterward they ordered more than they could eat at a swanky Italian restaurant.

They didn't get to bed until after 3:00 A.M., and then they made love for a particularly long time. Sally joked about the therapeutic effects of wine. After exchanging tender goodnight kisses, Carr dropped off into slumber.

During the night he reached over to touch Sally and she wasn't there. She came back to bed and was silent for several minutes, but Carr could tell by her breathing that she hadn't gone to sleep.

"Are you awake?" Sally finally whispered.

"Yes."

"We don't communicate on the same wavelength," she said. "We communicate in bed and when we're out and have had a few drinks. Other than that, you're like a stranger. You could be someone I sat next to on a bus. We've dated for years and I still truly do not understand you. Damn."

Carr fluffed a pillow. He leaned back against the headboard. "Let's get up and hit a couple of crap tables before we go back," he said. "We might get lucky."

"Please *communicate* with me, Charlie."

Carr rubbed his eyes for a moment. He sat up in bed. "We once stood in line in a Vegas parking lot in order to pay some clown fifty dollars to read marriage vows off a three-by-five card. But I couldn't go through with it. I don't want to buy a tract house. I don't want to join the P.T.A. I don't want to go to cocktail parties with the neighbors. I don't want to wear matching tennis shorts. I don't like picnics or Little League games . . ."

"In other words, you are a completely fulfilled person," she said. "You are satisfied with your life. Is that what you're saying?"

"No," Carr said in a low and serious tone. "It was about a year ago when I faced myself for the first time in my life. I woke up one morning and went to the breakfast table. It was cold in my apartment and I was alone. I thought about the fact that someday I was going to have to retire. And do you know what I said to myself?"

Sally sat up. "What?"

"I said, *It's time to start taking yoga lessons.* I never got around to taking them, mind you, but I thought seriously about it, and as a matter of fact, later that day I bought a quart of yogurt and mixed it with some bran flakes."

"You're making fun of me," Sally Malone said. Angrily, she threw the covers back and got out of bed. She fumbled with cigarettes and matches on a dresser table. "I'm sorry for having brought up anything more serious than a Dodger game," she said.

Carr reached out and grabbed her arm. He pulled her back into bed. As she protested, he covered her mouth with his.

In the morning they grabbed a quick breakfast and headed back to Los Angeles.

The airport was a swarming arena; everyone dragging trunks, suitcases, and children from place to place, shouting instructions to one another, waiting impatiently in lines.

Paul LaMonica dialed a number on the pay phone. He put a finger in the other ear to keep out the noise. A secretary connected him with Omar T. Lockhart. "I've spoken with my client," LaMonica said without introduction. "I'd like you to meet me at the Houston Airport, in the bar, as soon as possible. I'm waiting to catch a flight." *That will give you a chance to have someone follow me, you pig-eyed sonofabitch,* he thought.

There was a silence. "Okay," Lockhart said. "I'll be right down." He sounded annoyed.

LaMonica hung up the telephone. He went straight to a ticket counter, stood in line, and bought a ticket to San Diego. The clerk handed him the ticket and a boarding pass.

"You're all checked in, Mr. Ross," the clerk said. "We'll board in an hour."

The bar, situated on a balcony overlooking a maze of ticket counters, had few customers. LaMonica waited behind a bank of rental lockers until Lockhart picked out a table and sat down. A minute later a husky man with a shaved head sat down at the bar itself. He and Lockhart exchanged glances.

LaMonica strolled over to Lockhart's table and sat down without a greeting.

Lockhart spoke first. "My company doesn't like to involve itself in this sort of business," he said. A short-skirted waitress wearing a cowboy hat came to the table. They ordered Bloody Marys and the waitress walked away. "We're not jumping into anything half-cocked. You're going to have to give me some background details before we go any further."

"Be happy to," LaMonica said. "My client was the girl friend of Freddie Roth, a well-known counterfeiter. I say 'was' because Roth was murdered about a year ago in an underworld dispute. At the time of his death he had just finished printing two million dollars' worth of your precious traveler's checks. Apparently he had a European buyer for the whole batch. Anyway, my client is sitting on the checks, all of them, right now. That's the story in brief."

A wave of perspiration was evident on both of Lockhart's chins. He avoided looking toward the man at the bar. "Now I'll ask you the prize question," he said. "How much will she settle for?"

The waitress brought drinks. Lockhart took a healthy gulp and wiped his mouth with a napkin.

"Ten percent," LaMonica said.

"A hundred thousand dollars? You can go back and tell her flat out that **she**'s not going to get it. *Flat out. No way,*" Lockhart said.

LaMonica sipped his drink. "The *amount* of money she wants is not even the hard part," he said. "Freddie Roth's last printing job was contracted by the Mafia . . . yes, the actual honest-to-God Italian Mafia. If you check on Roth you'll see he was well connected. After Roth's murder, she tried to peddle some of the checks. They found out about it and sent some hoods to take the checks from her. My client heard they were coming, grabbed the checks, and went into hiding. She had planned to live by passing a few of the checks now and then—as you can see, they're of very high quality, easy to pass—but she got cold feet." LaMonica smiled "I don't know whether she was more afraid of the Mafia or the police."

"And just how did you get involved?" Lockhart asked.

"I do investigative work for her attorney," LaMonica said. "He asked me to check out her story; she owes him a sizable legal fee." He wiped condensation off the outside of his glass.

"We're not going to pay ten percent," Lockhart said. His chin dripped sweat. It seemed he had nothing else to say.

"I'll certainly relay that message to her," LaMonica said. "I just hope the Mafia won't pay ten percent either. She's negotiating with them, too, as you may have already guessed. As I understand it, *their* distribution problems are *minimum.*" He looked at his wristwatch. "I've got a flight to catch."

Lockhart nodded dumbly.

LaMonica got up and they shook hands. "I'll be back in touch," he said.

"I want to meet your client. I have to speak with her in person," Lockhart said as if mouthing his one and only line in the school play.

"I'll tell her that." LaMonica headed down an escalator and made his way to the boarding gates. At the intersection of two busy corridors, he hid behind a ticket-counter partition. Moments later the man with the shaved head rushed past him like a hound after a rabbit. LaMonica checked his watch once again, then trotted to a boarding area at the opposite end of the airport. He approached a gate and gave a red-suited boarding agent his ticket.

"You just made it, Mr. Ross," said the man. "Please hurry. The flight is ready to depart."

LaMonica rushed down the boarding ramp and onto the plane. He found his seat and fastened his seat belt.

The jumbo jet was only half full. In the seat next to him was a bespectacled young woman wearing designer jeans and a cashmere sweater. She was reading a thick book. Her gray-streaked hair was pulled back smartly. As the plane lifted off LaMonica leaned back and took a deep breath.

After a while, the woman put the book down and stretched. LaMonica smiled. She smiled back.

"Live in San Diego?" he said.

The woman shook her head. "Business trip."

"I love your sweater," he said. "In fact, I bought my wife one just like it. I was in New York at a medical convention and I missed her birthday. I feel just awful about it."

The woman smiled. "She'll forgive you. I take it you're a doctor?"

"Yes, I'm a neurosurgeon. My name is Bill Adams." They shook hands.

"Carol Williamson," she said. "I'm a buyer for a department store."

"I just hate to travel," he said. "I guess I'm kind of a homebody."

"I don't mind it so much," she said.

LaMonica closed his eyes. Later, he slid back in his seat and allowed Carol Williamson to step into the aisle. She found her way to the front of the cabin and entered the lavatory.

LaMonica looked around carefully. With one hand, he opened her purse and dug out a wallet. His fingers flew to the money pouch. About fifty dollars. Not worth the risk. He pulled two of the ten or so credit cards out of the wallet and pocketed them, then shoved the wallet back into the purse and shut it. He leaned back and closed his eyes again. When Carol Williamson returned and stepped gingerly around him, he acted as if he were asleep. As her leg brushed his he imagined grabbing her crotch with both hands and squeezing until she cried. She wiggled back into her seat.

When she tried to initiate some small talk, he ignored her.

Over the intercom the pilot announced the weather forecast for San Diego. By midnight LaMonica would be back across the border and at the safe house. He visualized himself lying on the cot—naked, secure and comfortable. Women (he recognized none of them) stood by the bed clutching rattan baskets overflowing with money. They nodded to one another and emptied the baskets over his body. Some of the money fell off the sides of the cot and onto the floor. He was immersed in crisp, rich greenbacks, unable to move, unable to touch himself.

CHAPTER 15

The floor of the huge jai-alai auditorium was a carpet of discarded betting tickets and empty beer cups, the refuse of a seedy-looking crowd (at least half were Americans) that milled around the betting windows. The electronic tote boards at either end of the fronton flashed changing odds on the Perfecta, Quiniela, and Trifecta combinations, gambling jargon designed to avoid the use of the word *lose*.

The court itself was an enormous well-lit stage shielded by fine netting. On its left side half a dozen bored-looking Mexican men sat in a cagelike affair waiting to compete. They were dressed in white trousers and colorful shirts.

Paul LaMonica found Sandy sitting alone in the reserved section. He plopped down in a seat next to her. "They want to meet you," he said.

"Are they suspicious?" She turned the page of the program she was reading.

"A little. You can't blame them. There's a lot of money involved," LaMonica said in a confident tone.

Sandy closed the program and stared at the court. "I don't like showing my face. It scares the shit out of me to show my face," she said.

"No U.S. soil, no U.S. crime," LaMonica said.

"But they could put us together behind a conspiracy."

"So what's another grain of sand on the beach?" La-Monica said.

The players marched to the middle of the court and bowed to scattered applause. Two of them strutted to the service line while the rest returned to the cage. The game began.

"They're no better than the greyhounds who chase the mechanical rabbit," Sandy said, her eyes on the court, "or racehorses. They just come out like slaves and perform. Sad, don't you think?"

"I'm sure they're not too sad in the locker room every night when they sit around and cut up the side bets," La-Monica said. "Racehorses with brains."

"I hope they don't ask me too much about this Freddie Roth person," Sandy said.

"If they do, you just play it by ear—keep everything vague."

The pelota slammed against the front wall like a rifle shot. It bounced back full court. A player was waiting. He caught the ball and roundhoused it back.

"Mr. Cool keeps asking me about you," she said. "He's afraid you're going to rip me off." Sandy gave him a funny smile.

"Your *main man*," LaMonica said sarcastically.

"We're just using each other," Sandy said. "Just like you and I always have."

"I don't like him."

"You don't like *anyone*. Particularly black people. You've always been that way."

They didn't speak again until the first game was over. The number-three player had beaten number seven with a kill shot to the corner.

"I want you to keep your Mr. Cool out of this," LaMonica said. "What you do with him on your own is your business. You and I had something once, but that's over now. I have no jealousy."

"You never had any kind of feelings," she said, her eyes on the fronton.

LaMonica ignored the remark. "I have a good feeling about our *thing*. And I'm positive that we'll be able to get it done if we can just keep the program simple and avoid getting other people involved. These things have a tendency to draw outsiders. They smell the bucks at the end of the line. We must avoid letting anyone else in on our act. The risk is too great."

"You always keep everything to yourself," she said. "For the whole year we were together I never had any idea where we were going or what we were going to do from one day to the next. I realized it after the cops grabbed me in Las Vegas. They asked me where we were planning to hit next. I actually had no idea." She gave a little laugh. "Hell, even if I'd *wanted* to do myself a favor and be a rat, I couldn't. You never let me in on the planning. We did live high for that year, though; I will say that. We lived real high."

"I want us to be partners in this," LaMonica said. "Don't forget. If things get heavy it'll be you and me against the wall. We can't let other people in on *any* of the details. There's too much at stake. You should realize that. It's a chance for us to get out of this border act once and for all—to head for Europe, Australia, with a whole new identity. To me, being stuck down here with these bean bandits is as bad as being in the joint."

"I hear you," Sandy said.

It was payday. Ling's was crowded and noisy.

The platoon of federal cops glued to the bar barked for more drinks like kenneled dogs. Ling sat on the floor in the corner of the place probing a broken jukebox with a long screwdriver.

"Chickenshit service! Chickenshit service!" chanted the bar revelers. Ling stood up and pointed to the ancient machine with the screwdriver.

"You want this thing fix?" he said angrily.

Shouts of "Fuck the jukebox!"

Jack Kelly hoisted his empty glass like a knight's banner. "And fuck all your moth-eaten Frank Sinatra and Jerry

Vale records!" he said. There was a violent round of laughter.

Ling tossed the screwdriver on the floor and huffed back to the bar. The laughter continued as he filled glasses with ice. He grabbed one of the glasses, rubbed it on his butt, and held it up. "This one for you, Kelly." The laughter was deafening.

Carr sat in a booth with Frank Garcia. Garcia was dressed "TJ" fashion: a cowboy-style shirt and boots, like the million or so Mexicans who filled L.A.'s run-down apartments and garment-district sweatshops. He was thirtyish but looked older because of his rheumy eyes.

"When are you going to move in on Shorty McFadden?" Carr said.

"Don't ask me," Garcia said. "I'm on a thirty-day suspension." His barrio accent was slurred from liquor. "The other night I stopped after work for a few drinks. I'd just finished working sixteen hours straight. I hadn't eaten all day, so the booze hits me. I walk out of the bar and realize I'm so drunk I can't drive home, so I hop in the backseat of my car and try to catch a few winks. I figured that if I slept for a while, I'd sober up enough to drive." He sipped his drink and stirred the ice. "Next thing I know, a couple of blue-suiters are pulling me out of the car. I show 'em my federal tin, but they don't believe me. They think it's stolen. They actually throw the cuffs on me and take me to the police station! Like there I am getting my *fingerprints* taken. I'm getting *booked* for being drunk in public. Luckily, one of the narcs in the station recognizes me and I get cut loose, but it's too late. The blue-suiters have already called up my agent in charge to verify my credentials." He finished his drink and slammed the glass down. "So I end up with thirty days no pay. Can you imagine that? Thirty days on the beach for not wanting to drive drunk!" He shook his head sadly. "Things like that happen to me all the time."

Carr gave him a sympathetic look. "Not to change the subject, but didn't you pull some capers below the border last year?" he said.

"I was on loan to Immigration. They sent me down there four times last year," Garcia said. "In Tijuana I'd pay a *coyote* two hundred bucks from the confidential fund and then just take the trip. Sometimes it was in the bed of a truck, sometimes stuffed like a sardine in the back of a van or camper. It would be a full-blown surveillance all the way from the border into Los Angeles. I'd give the signal at the drop-off point and we'd arrest everybody, a conspiracy case usually. The illegal aliens would get deported and the *coyotes* would bail out and slip back across the border. They'd be back in business before I finished writing my reports. The whole investigation ended up bringing in nothing more than a few extra fugitives."

"Where do the American fugitives hang out down there?" Carr said.

Garcia sipped his drink as if it were delicious soup. "Ensenada, probably. I've heard rumbles that there's a bar down there a lot of 'em go to. Rodriguez at the Ensenada Police Department keeps an eye on the Americans down there. He's a friend." He gave a quick glance around the bar, leaned close to Carr, and whispered, "And I hear the fanbelt inspectors have a caper going down there right now. It's some kind of a long-range operation. They're gathering information on the activities of American fugitives hiding in Mexico. They're paying some high-power snitch big money to find out who's who and what's what." He sat back and stopped whispering. "You know, one of those big idea things that will end up in a stack of bullshit FBI reports." Garcia chuckled.

"The kind of reports that will get passed around at organized-crime task-force meetings," Carr said. "Everyone will act like they recognize the names." He smiled.

"Maybe they'll call it Operation Bad-Ass Gringos," Garcia said, still laughing.

Car shook his head. "I'm afraid that code name wouldn't fly for them," he said. "Bad words."

Ling finally brought more drinks. He plunked them down and rushed away.

"On my last Mexico case I was stuffed in the back of a truck with so many people I damn near suffocated," Garcia said. "When the arrests finally went down, I told 'em I wasn't going to do it anymore. I've got a wife and five kids. You know what they said? They said I had job stress and they sent me to talk to a psychologist. He kept asking whether I felt tired all the time. I told him I never get tired. He asked me why I drink, how I get along with my wife sexually, crap like that. I told him it was none of his god-damn business. They don't know what to do with me now."

A tall man in a pin-striped suit walked in the front door. He took a seat at the end of the bar, making no effort to greet anyone.

"That's the FBI agent in charge of the fugitive operation I was telling you about," Garcia whispered. "His name is Tom Luegner. But he won't give you any information. You know how those people are."

Carr nodded. A while later he carried his drink to the bar and sat down next to Luegner. He introduced himself.

"I've seen you around," Luegner said. "You're a . . . uh . . . friend of Sally Malone." His smile exuded poise. Every hair on his head was in place, the knot in his tie of a perfect size and shape.

Carr ignored the remark. "One of my informants was murdered by a federal fugitive named Paul LaMonica," Carr said. "LaMonica supposedly lives in Mexico. I could use some help."

Luegner tore off the corner of his cocktail napkin. He rolled it between his fingers. "The name does kind of ring a bell," he said. "What was your informant's name?"

"Linda Gleason," Carr said. Would you like me to spell it for your report? he thought.

"And LaMonica killed her?" Luegner said.

"That's right."

"I'd sure like to help you out," Luegner said in an off-handed manner. "But you know how sensitive our intelli-gence files are. Of course it's no secret that we've had reports that LaMonica has been seen now and then below the border." Without saying excuse me, Luegner reached in front of Carr and grabbed a few bar olives. He plopped them in his martini.

Carr felt the blood rushing to his face. "You can't blame me for trying," he said in a self-deprecating manner.

Luegner smiled. "Certainly not. We're all in the same business."

Carr stood up. He finished his drink and set the glass down on the bar.

Luegner stuffed an olive in his mouth. "By the way," he said as he chewed, "seen Sally lately?"

"As a matter of fact I haven't," Carr said casually. He waved at Kelly and strolled out the door.

Carr headed down a pedestrian walkway lined with souvenir shops, which because of the hour were closed. He stopped at the entrance to a small parking lot. There were no more than ten vehicles. A silver Corvette was parked in the corner of the dimly lit area next to a commercial trash receptacle. Carr sauntered over to the Corvette. He pulled a pen-sized flashlight out of his coat pocket, flicked it on, and ran the beam of light along the interior of the vehicle. There was a gasoline credit-card receipt on the front seat bearing Tom Luegner's name. He flicked the light off and stepped to the trash bin. Using the light, he rummaged around until he found a wire coat hanger. He pulled it out and twisted it straight, leaving a hook at the end.

Carr glanced around the lot again. He was still alone. Holding the flashlight in his teeth, he wedged the wire between window and doorframe. After four or five tries, he managed to maneuver the hook under the door handle. He tugged, the lock snapped, and he swung open the door and climbed in. Frantically, he dug around behind the front seat until he found what he was looking for—a heavy briefcase. Pulling it onto his lap, he tore at the latches and it popped open. Using the flashlight to read by, Carr flipped through a stack of reports titled "Informant Contact Report" and stamped CONFIDENTIAL.

Someone was crossing the lot.

Carr flicked off the flashlight and ducked down in the seat. He held his breath. The footsteps of more than one person. They came closer. Car doors opened. Men laughed. Car doors closed. A vehicle drove off.

Carr exhaled. Balancing the flashlight on his lap, he raced through the papers as fast as he could. The report that caught his attention was the one with the most recent date. It was written in the standard FBI format:

TO: Special Agent in Charge
FROM: Assistant to the Special Agent in Charge
        Thomas A. Luegner
Subject: Operation Peter Rabbit
Source: 2034XD
Method of Contact: Tel/con

Info: 2034XD reports that fugitive Sandra Hartz-
      becker aka Sandra Hill (FBI #5658940H) met
      recently in Ensenada with a male adult identi-
      fied as Paul LaMonica (FBI #9586744L) for
      the purpose of planning early stages of a state-
      side forgery scheme. No further information.
      Rec checks show LaMonica subject of fug.
      warrant #bhk5906 for escape. Subject escaped
      from Terminal Island federal prison eleven
      months ago after overpowering a civilian em-
      ployee at the institution. He used a counterfeit
      police identification card to facilitate his
      escape. Subject is a master printer, many
      times convicted of counterfeiting U.S. cur-
      rency, various types of checks, etc. No further
      information. Hartzbecker is former girl friend/
      criminal cohort (counterfeit money passer) of
      LaMonica.

Undeveloped leads: Maintain contact with Source.

Carr slammed the briefcase shut and set it in the back-seat exactly as he'd found it. He slipped out of the Corvette, closed the door quietly, and tossed the coat hanger back into the trash can.

Carr climbed into his sedan and started the engine. On the way to his apartment he listened to an all-night jazz station.

CHAPTER 16

In the morning Carr found the arrest folder in the bottom drawer of a filing cabinet marked "Closed Cases." A tab on the folder read "Hartzbecker, Sandra/Passer." He carried the folder to a desk in the corner of the room and sat down. He opened the folder. There was nothing inside it except some mug shots. Hartzbecker was dressed in a well-tailored pants suit and her hair was in pigtails. Like everyone in such photographs, she wore a frown.

Carr flipped the stack of mug shots over. Each photo was stamped FIELD FILE ON THIS SUSPECT STORED IN THE LAS VEGAS FIELD OFFICE. He flipped the folder shut. There was a phone on the desk. He picked up the receiver and dialed.

"U.S. Treasury. Las Vegas Field Office, Special Agent Cecil True speaking. Good morning." The agent ran the words together as if reciting Hail Mary number twenty.

"This is Charlie," Carr said. "I need a little info."

"I hope you liked my introduction," True said. "I got written up last week for answering the phone, 'Treasury.'"

"Do you remember a passer named Sandra Hartzbecker?" Carr asked.

There was a momentary silence. "That's a roger," True

GERALD PETIEVICH

said. "German broad . . . fifty-dollar notes; the pinch went down in the Casino Monte Carlo."

"What happened?" Carr said.

"She was playing craps at one of the high-stakes tables dropping fifty-dollar bills for chips. The pit boss at the table takes a look at one of the bills and gets suspicious. He calls security and they try to put the arm on her. The fight is on. She scratched the shit out of one of the guards. By the time I got there it was all over but the shouting."

"Did she talk?" Carr said.

"Nope," True said. "She did the 'I cashed a check at a bank in L.A.' act. At the Field Office I poured her purse out on the desk right in front of her. There's nothing in it but counterfeit fifties and a motel key. Of course she said she'd never seen the key before. I put her in the lockup and headed down to the motel. There was about fifty grand in the same variety of fifties in a shoebox hidden under the bed as well as a couple of pairs of men's pants and shirts hanging in the closets along with her stuff. Back at the office I showed her the shoebox and she started crying. Never would cop out on her boyfriend, though. She's really a solid broad. I figured it out anyway. She had an address book in her purse. I can't remember the guy's name right offhand . . ."

"Paul LaMonica?" Carr said.

"That's it," True said. "I really pressed her, even offered her a deal if she would hand him up, but she stuck by her guns. She kept her story all the way to the joint. A solid broad. Ya gotta give her credit."

"Thanks for the rundown," Carr said.

"Anytime," True said. "By the way, how's our old buddy No Waves?"

"About the same," Carr said.

"That's why I like it right here in good ol' Las Vegas." True cleared his voice. "U.S. Treasury Las Vegas Field Office, Special Agent True signing off. Have a real nice day," he said in a sarcastic tone.

Carr smiled and shook his head. He hung up the receiver.

It was almost midnight. LaMonica had been catnapping in an overstuffed chair.

The light and sound of a television set filled the hotel room, a talk show featuring a youthful cowboy actor with plucked eyebrows rambling on about the dangers of nuclear power. There was nothing else on.

Like the other cubicles on the top floor of the Tijuana Excelsior, the room was replete with fancy tilework and imitation primitive art. LaMonica rose from the chair and stretched. He stabbed his way through sheer curtains to the spacious balcony.

Sandy, resting on one of the two double beds, remained transfixed by the television.

The view from the balcony was partially obstructed by the downtown bullring, an ominous structure that loomed liked some ancient ruin. To the right, American Border Patrol helicopters with powerful spotlights rattled along north of the international boundary searching for intruders. A breeze, tepid and gusting steadily, came from that direction.

"Would you like to go over it again?" LaMonica said to the wind.

"What?" Sandy said. The bed creaked. She went to the dressing table and poured a drink.

"Go over it again," he said, raising his voice.

Sandy pushed her way through the curtain and stood next to him. She held a drink. "If I don't have it down by now I never will," she said between sips.

A helicopter descended suddenly, its beam of light aimed at something moving on the ground. Vehicle lights sped along the fence. After a while the helicopter ascended and followed the border east. Finally it was out of sight.

"Funny, the two of us spending the night together," Sandy said. "After that last time I swore I'd never work with you again. And here we are rehearsing an act."

"I wanted you in on this. I really did," LaMonica said. His hands held the balcony rail.

"I'm here because I finally said to myself that if you really did rip me off in that last thing, you would never have had the guts to ask me to work with you again," Sandy said. "Plus, I sort of respect you . . . the way you work alone and take care of business. You're not a bullshit artist. And because I have a chance to make enough money to change everything for once and for all. I want *out* of this fuckin' place. It's a goal." She held the drink to her forehead.

"What about your boyfriend, *Mr. Cool?*" LaMonica said. "You'd just leave him behind?" He smirked.

"I once read in a women's-lib book that women should have relationships with lower-class men in order to develop confidence," Sandy Hartzbecker said. "I think the author was right. My relationship with Mr. Cool has changed me. I feel different after having been with him. He's his own man, but he's concerned about what happens to me. We're equals. We respect each other and always have something to talk about. We share things and look out for one another. The book was right. Fuck what other people think." Her expression was one of disdain.

"If Lockhart puts you on the spot tomorrow, just turn on the tears and leave the room," LaMonica said. "I'll follow you out and then we'll decide what to do next. We have to play it by ear. On the other hand, don't be afraid to push him to the wall. I read him as basically a pussy. He'll cave in with pressure. Even if he tells us to shove it and walks out, don't worry. We can always go back later with a lower offer."

Like a ritual of good luck, they went over the details again. By the time they'd hashed it all out, Sandy had downed three more drinks. They went back into the room and got undressed.

Sandy fluffed a pillow and flopped down on her bed. LaMonica climbed onto the other bed and flicked off the light on the nightstand. There was only moonlight in the room. It was too warm for covers.

"You wanted me in the same room with you so I couldn't back out at the last minute," Sandy said. Her speech was slightly slurred from the drinks. "You're a great one for details. You like to have everything just right. Just the way *you* want it . . . even in sex."

A gust of wind. The curtains reached into the room like ghost's hands. A sound in the distance might have been a siren. They stirred for a while. Nothing was said.

"I'll do it if you want me to," Sandy said flatly. "I can't sleep."

"I'd like that," LaMonica said.

"Only if we can start my way," she said. "There's a jar in my purse."

LaMonica reached into the purse on the nightstand. He removed a jar of surgical jelly.

Sandy rolled over and adjusted a pillow under her stomach. "When I say stop, I mean stop."

Sitting on the balcony with the morning sun warming his back, Paul LaMonica felt encouraged. The plan had progressed. He knew Omar T. Lockhart had not waddled all the way from Texas to Tijuana just to shoot the shit.

For over an hour the topic of discussion had been money. There had been first and second offers, and the hotel room was filled with fiery talk about them. Sandy Hartzbecker, wearing a jumpsuit, paced around the room puffing on brown cigarettes, making demands. For emphasis, now and then she would aim a finger at Lockhart as if it were a gun.

Lockhart looked perfectly uncomfortable sitting at a table. He clicked furiously on a ballpoint pen.

"A hundred thousand dollars is completely out of the question," Lockhart said, bobbing his puffy head in a bow of confidence. "We'd just as soon take our chances and let the damn checks get distributed and passed. Sure, we'll sustain some loss, but the police will catch the forgers eventually." He leaned back in the rattan chair.

Sandy was perched on the edge of the bed facing the balcony. She stabbed a finger in the direction of the fat man's face. "Then you can go right ahead and do just that!" she said. "Because if you think I'm going to settle for one dime less, you're crazy. I came to you people because I wanted to do the right thing . . . and because of what those Mafia bastards did to my Freddie." Her voice was filled with emotion. She sniffled. Tear action. "But I swear to God I'll sell the package to them unless I get enough money to make a new life for myself. They killed Freddie and they'll kill me if they don't get the checks. I'm going to need a new identity, a new life. These things cost money." She pulled a tissue from a box and wiped her nose.

Lockhart leaned back in the chair. His neck disappeared in the burden of flesh under his chin. "I hope you realize that simple possession of those counterfeit checks is a felony violation of law," he said smugly.

"Oh, so now you want to *threaten* me?" Sandy said. "Then why don't you just go ahead and call the FBI! Or the cops or the Secret Service or whoeverthefuck you want to call. This is *Mexico*, you sonofabitch! U.S. laws don't apply here!" Sandy grabbed more tissues. She dabbed her eyes furiously.

"There's no need to raise your voice," said Lockhart without any show of emotion. "I receive my instructions from a board of directors. There are certain ground rules that I—"

"Then go back and tell your board of directors to get *fucked!*" Sandy jumped to her feet. "I have nothing else to say to you. I've made up my mind to go the other way." More loud sniffles as she rushed to the door. She swung it open.

"I am prepared to make a final substantial offer," Lockhart said, "if you would care to listen."

Sandy's hands were on her hips. "Then make it," she said.

Lockhart blinked rapidly before he spoke. "Twenty-five thousand dollars for full recovery."

Sandy's hands flew to her face. Sobs. She ran out of the room.

LaMonica shook his head in mock despair. "I'll get her," he said on his way out of the room.

Sandy was pacing back and forth in front of the elevators.

LaMonica put his arm around her shoulder just in case anyone was watching. They strolled slowly along the corridor.

"What the hell do I do now?" she whispered.

LaMonica looked up and down the hall. "Counter-offer with fifty thousand and don't come off it," he said. "Give him three days to make up his mind."

LaMonica led her back into the room. She sat down on the bed again. Lockhart stood on the balcony. His face was damp, oily.

"Those people will put a contract out on me if they don't get the checks," Sandy said, wiping a tear. "They'll come after me. That means I won't be able to work at a regular job or go anywhere near my friends or family. I'm probably stupid for not giving them the checks and having it over and done with . . . but I hate them. My Freddie would turn over in his grave." Her hands wiped tears from her eyes. "I need at least fifty thousand. I need it because I have four kids. I can't work. We'll have to move." Her eyes sought the ceiling. "I wish to God I had never seen the damn checks."

Lockhart stood up. He hoisted his trousers over the mound that was his belly. "We're not able to pay any more than I have offered. I'm sorry," he said.

"That's final," Sandy said. "If that's the way you people feel about me, then the hell with it! Day after tomorrow I'm turning the checks over to the Italians. It's worth a hundred grand to avoid the death sentence!" She cupped her face in her hands and sobbed.

Omar Lockhart waddled to the door and opened it wide. "I'm sorry," he said. He walked out, closing the door gently behind him.

Sandy waved an extended middle finger at the door. LaMonica grabbed her arm and swung her to him. His hand closed over her mouth. His lips were at her ear. "Don't say a word," he whispered. She stared at LaMonica with a look of fear as he released her arm and picked up the chair Lockhart had been sitting in. LaMonica turned it over and examined it closely, then set it down without making a sound. Dropping to his knees, he searched under the table next to it. He motioned to her and she joined him under the table. He pointed to a black object the size of a dime. It was fastened under the rim of the table with a gumlike substance.

They crawled out from underneath the table and stood up. LaMonica took a pen and pad out of his pocket and wrote, "Cry for a while, then tell me your mind is made up about the fifty thousand. Make up a story about how much debt you're in after Freddie's death, and so on." He showed her the note. The sobs began.

They did not check out of the room for over an hour.

CHAPTER 17

The stocky bald man waiting in the Treasury Field Office reception area wore an expensive-looking blue suit. There were grease spots on his silk necktie. Carr introduced himself, and the man handed him a business card.

It read:

OMAR T. LOCKHART

DIRECTOR OF SECURITY

TRAVELERS CHEX, INCORPORATED

HOUSTON, TEXAS

They shook hands.

"The secretary checked a name for me in your files . . . Freddie Roth," Lockhart said in a panhandle drawl. "She said you handled the case."

Carr nodded. "Roth is dead," he said. "Murdered over a year ago."

"That's a ten-four," Lockhart said. "And how was he killed, if I may ask?"

"Head blown off," Carr said. "Underworld dispute over

some counterfeit bonds he had printed. Why are you interested in old Freddie?'

"It's a confidential matter," said Lockhart. "Can you tell me anything about Freddie's young girl friend?"

Carr shrugged. "Have no idea. I know he used to live with a gal in El Monte."

"Did Roth ever print any counterfeit checks?" Lockhart asked. The look on his face was extremely inquisitive.

"Yep," Carr said. "Printed anything he could get a sample of. Did it his whole life. Checks, money, bonds, passports—you name it."

"Would you mind if I took a look at your file on Roth?" Lockhart said.

"Yes, I would mind," Carr said. "Particularly since you don't seem to want to tell me what this is all about."

"Sorry," said the fat man. "I just can't do that at this point."

"Then it's been nice talking with you." Carr turned, walked back into the office, and sat down at his desk. He continued thumbing through a stack of intelligence reports and initialing each page as required by the agent in charge.

Kelly looked up from his newspaper. "Who was that?"

"A private eye. He wanted some info on Freddie Roth," Carr said.

Kelly grunted. He folded the sports page.

The telephone rang and Carr picked up the receiver. It was Calhoun. "A white boy just showed me a sample twenty. I told him to come back in an hour. You'd better get on down here." The telephone clicked.

"Calhoun's got one," Carr said. He stood up and shrugged on his suit jacket. Kelly folded the newspaper and stuffed it into his coat pocket. He followed Carr out the door.

Carr steered north on Vermont Avenue toward Hollywood. At a stop light Kelly finished reading his newspaper, then tossed it in the backseat. "I hate this paper," he said. "The editorials are antipolice." He turned to Carr. "Ever ask yourself why?"

"Why what?"

"Why a newspaper would be against the police?"

"No," Carr said. His mind was on the chalk outline of Linda's body on the floor of her living room.

"It's because the editors are out-and-out Communists," Kelly said.

Charles Carr drove slowly by Calhoun's hot-dog stand. There were no customers. He pulled over to the curb two doors up. Leaving the keys in the ignition, he climbed out of the sedan and sauntered back to Calhoun's counter.

Calhoun spoke as if he were out of breath. "This white boy wanted to sell me five hundred bucks' worth of twenties for a hundred-dollar bill. I told him to come back in an hour with the whole package. That was forty minutes ago."

"Who is he?"

"I don't know his name," Calhoun said. "I always called him Curly. He used to be hanging around here. I think he was dealing weed. A couple of months ago he must've made hisself a real good score. He started driving a sports car and I seen him with a blonde. A good-looking gal with a nice ass."

"What does he look like?"

"Curly hair and sort of a peach-fuzz beard. I figured him for a user because he's always sniffling his nose and sometimes he wears a long-sleeved shirt even when it's hot as hell. He drives a white Porsche."

Carr gave a knowing nod.

"You know the muthafucka?"

"I think so," Carr said. "Kelly and I will be across the street in that alley." He pointed. "Once you see the funny money, give us a wave. Tell him you don't like the quality and you're not interested. When he leaves, we'll follow."

Calhoun winked.

Carr returned to the sedan. He climbed in and started the engine. As he pulled into an alley facing the hot-dog stand, he told Kelly what he'd just learned. Minutes later the young man in the white Porsche pulled up in front of Calhoun's. He exited the Porsche and headed for the counter carrying a brown paper sack. After speaking briefly with Calhoun, he handed over the bag. Calhoun opened it, looked inside, and handed it back. As the young man stuffed the sack under his shirt, Calhoun's fingers made a discreet wave.

Charles Carr started the engine. The young man gestured angrily at Calhoun, then shook his head in a disgusted manner and shuffled back to the Porsche. As he drove north on Vermont, Charles Carr pulled into traffic a half block behind the sports car.

"If he sees us, he'll throw his package," Kelly said.

Carr nodded. The Porsche turned right on Hollywood Boulevard. Carr stepped on the gas and made the same turn. The streets were crowded with the usual mixture of tourists and leather freaks, teenage whores, men dressed as women, and muggers of all races. It seemed that everyone wore sunglasses.

"We're far enough away," Carr said. "Let's do it."

Kelly reached under the seat and pulled out a red light with a magnetic bottom. He plugged it into the cigarette lighter. The red light flashed. With a hook-shot reach, he mounted it on the roof of the sedan. The Porsche accelerated and swerved right onto a residential street. As the driver tossed the brown bag out the window, Carr braked sharply. Kelly swung open the passenger door and retrieved the bag.

Carr floored the accelerator. The Porsche's tires squealed as it rounded another corner onto a busy street. The Porsche was almost a block ahead as the G-car made the turn. It swerved to avoid a double-parked truck and sideswiped a station wagon coming from the other direction. The Porsche vaulted a curb and crashed into the side of an apartment house.

Carr slammed on the brakes. The T-men jumped out of the sedan and approached the sports car with guns drawn. The driver struggled frantically to start the engine. Carr swung open the door and yanked the man out by his hair. Kelly frisked him and snapped on the handcuffs.

"How long have you been following me?" he said.

"All day," Carr said. Kelly led the man back to the sedan.

After the arrival of tow trucks and police cars, and the signing of various forms, they proceeded to the Field Office with the prisoner.

"I can help you guys out again if you will do something for me," the young man said.

"We're listening," said Kelly, who was sitting in the back seat next to him.

Carr steered onto the freeway toward downtown.

"I think I know who the printer is."

"Who is it?" Kelly said.

"What'll you do for me?" he said.

Nothing was said for a while. The freeway signs read "Broadway," "Los Angeles Street." Carr steered onto an off ramp and headed down a hill toward the Federal Building.

"The printer's name is Paulie and he's a friend of Teddy Mora. He lives down in Ensenada. That's what I heard."

"Have you ever met him?" Carr said.

"No. I've just heard talk."

"Thanks a lot for the tip," Kelly said.

"I guess that means you're not going to give me a break," the young man said.

"That's right," Kelly said.

"I wanna see my lawyer."

Carr and Kelly spent the next few hours on the usual processing: taking fingerprints, filling out forms, preparing affidavits and reports. It was dark by the time they booked their prisoner into the Los Angeles County jail.

Early the next morning Carr and Kelly met in the reception area of the United States attorney's office, a handsomely carpeted room decorated with framed photographs of the president, the attorney general, and the latest U.S. attorney, a former local presidential campaign manager. During the hour they spent waiting, the receptionist, a redhaired woman wearing a shapeless polka-dot dress, phoned her mother, painted and blew-dry her fingernails, phoned a friend and discussed a television program, thumbed through a movie magazine, and painstakingly switched stations on a tiny transistor radio several times.

Finally, Reba Partch, wearing a white skirt and sweater with yellowed underarms, hustled in the front door carrying a large straw purse in one hand and a hairbrush in the other. She applied brush strokes to her dandruffy Brillo pad as she strode to the receptionist's desk. The receptionist handed her some phone-message slips and nodded at Carr and Kelly. Partch glanced at the T-men as if they were mannequins. She flicked dandruff off her shoulders and proceeded to her office.

Half an hour later the receptionist's phone rang. She answered it, then set down the receiver. "You can go in now," she said.

Carr and Kelly headed down a hallway. They stepped into Partch's office. She was on the phone. They sat down. On the wall behind her was hung a USC diploma and a framed photograph of Partch and three other equally unattractive young women wearing T-shirts and jeans. They were sitting in a rubber raft next to a dock. Everyone held up beer cans.

"Gotta run," Partch said and hung up the phone.

Carr started to speak. Partch held up her hand, then dialed the phone again. "Service department, please," she said. After a lengthy discussion concerning shock absorbers and how much she needed her car by tonight, she hung up.

Carr started to speak again.

"Reports," she said as she made a "gimme" motion with her hands.

Carr bit his lip and handed her the reports. She stuffed a handful of cough drops into her mouth and rattled them around against her teeth as she read. Having turned all the pages, she handed the reports back. "Lack of sufficient evidence to prove criminal intent," she said.

"Even though he threw the counterfeit money out the window of his car when he saw us following him?" Carr said.

"In court he could take the witness stand and say that he thought the bag contained narcotics or some other such contraband. Without some proof that the defendant knew that the bag contained counterfeit money as opposed to any other kind of illegal goods, the judge would throw the case out. The counterfeiting statutes require proof of *specific* criminal intent. As usual, your case is weak because you won't reveal your informants." She made a smile similar to the one in the raft picture. "So you'll have to release your prisoner."

Charles Carr took back the reports and folded them. He and Kelly stood up.

Reba Partch said, "Any questions?"

Without a word, Carr and Kelly headed out of the office to the elevator. The elevator door opened and they stepped inside. Partch rushed out after them. She posed angrily with her hands on her hips. "Must you people really be so *rude?*" Kelly pushed the elevator button and the door closed. They returned to the Field Office without discussing the incident.

CHAPTER 18

There was the smell of coffee in the board room. The executives drank the beverage without clinking their cups. All, including Omar T. Lockhart, avoided the neat piles of sweet rolls. It was the usual Wednesday meeting, attendance mandatory, fresh notepads in front of every handsome leather chair.

Lockhart responded to the chairman's nod by sitting up in his chair. He opened a folder full of typed memoranda. "I've completed the preliminary negotiations," he said. "It's going to take sweetening the pot some from our offer of twenty-five thousand, but I'm convinced we'll be able to buy the checks." He had practiced saying this.

Every eye in the room was on him. Lockhart prayed that he wouldn't break into one of his uncontrollable sweats.

The chairman uncapped his gold ink pen and scribbled on a pad. "Number one," he said, "I'll authorize fifty thousand to 'sweeten the pot,' as you put it. Not a cent more. Number two, we'll not be going to Mexico for the final transaction. It's too dangerous. They will have to come to meet us on U.S. soil. Number three, just who in the hell are these folks?" He looked up.

Lockhart cleared his throat. "I've been able to develop

some valuable information along those lines. I checked police records and visited the Los Angeles office of the U.S. Treasury Department—"

"And what have you learned?" the chairman interrupted, his tone impatient.

Lockhart's neck and forehead suddenly felt damp. He referred to his memoranda. "Uh, I've learned that there was, in fact, a Freddie Roth and that Roth was a convicted counterfeiter of checks, bonds, and currency. Roth was murdered by another underworld type a year or so ago. At this point it hasn't been established whether he had a girl friend. He was married you see, and this was probably something he would try to hide from his wife . . ."

The chairman of the board frowned. "I find the whole matter disgusting," he said.

Everyone at the long table gave concerned nods.

"Let's move on to the next item on the agenda," he said.

The phone rang.

Carr sat up in bed. He snatched the receiver off the nightstand.

"Why didn't you call me?" the woman said. "You said you would."

"I've been busy." He had no idea who she was.

"I've heard that one before," she said, "but please don't think that you just got lucky in the middle of the night. I don't call men. They have to call me."

Carr rubbed his eyes. He had a headache.

"You really have no idea who this is, do you?" she said.

Carr didn't answer.

"The reason I called is that a dyke just got booked here for attempted murder and she says she has some information for you. Her name is"—there was the rustling of papers—"Rosanna DuMaurier. Her a.k.a. is Rosemary Cramp."

Carr forced himself to open his eyes. "I'll be right down," he said. "Uh, thanks for the call."

The phone clicked. Carr staggered out of bed and into the shower. He turned on the cold water and groaned as it startled him into consciousness. Having dressed, he headed for the L.A. women's jail. By the time he reached City Terrace Drive and accelerated up the hill, it was daybreak. After parking his car in the visitor's lot, he approached a large guard booth and held up his badge and I.D. card to the glass. The gate in front of him buzzed, and he pushed it open. Carr took a familiar path along a cement courtyard toward the visiting room. He passed through another set of doors, then followed a yellow line on the floor down a corridor to a window made of bulletproof glass. A blonde in a tight-fitting khaki uniform sat behind the window. She was close to his age and had a sheriff's gold badge mounted on her left breast. She made a kiss movement at him.

"Remember me now?" she said. "Chinatown on payday night? Bob Tomsic, the Secret Service agent, was with my girl friend. She was wearing the Mickey Mouse T-shirt." Her voice emanated from a speaker below the window.

"Of course I remember," Carr said in a tone of sincerity. "Who booked Rosemary?"

"L.A.P.D." she said. "A couple of Hollywood patrol officers. I know one of them. He told me she stabbed her girl friend through the arm with a vegetable knife. She was hysterical when she came in, but she's calmed down now. She begged me to call you, said you'd know what it was all about." The deputy pressed a button. A hydraulic lock snapped, and a steel door to Carr's left slid slowly open. The blond deputy made another kiss and offered a laconic smile. Carr smiled back. He stepped into a room full of long, Formica-covered tables. A few minutes later Rosemary Cramp, wearing a prisoner's denim sack dress, opened a door stenciled INMATES. She shuffled to the table and sat down across from him.

"Sorry to hear about your problem," Carr said.

"Are you still interested in finding Paul LaMonica?" she asked.

"Yes."

"If I tell you where you can find him, what will you do for me?" she said tersely.

"What do you *want* done for you?" Carr rubbed his temples. The hangover would not go away.

"I was booked on attempted murder," she said. "I want the charge dropped to assault with a deadly weapon. That's all I'm asking."

"What kind of injuries on the victim?" Carr said.

Rosemary Cramp's chin quivered. Deftly she used an index finger to wipe a tear out of each eye. "The whole thing was a misunderstanding. She was high. We were arguing over someone and she threw a clock radio and just missed my head. I grabbed a knife. I don't remember what happened exactly. All she has are a few cuts on her arms." She looked at the ceiling for a moment.

"I can talk to the D.A. and to the judge if you're convicted . . . let 'em know you cooperated on a case," Carr said. "Of course you know that's no guarantee that anything can be done."

She folded her hands and stared at them. "You can find Paul LaMonica at a bar called Teddy's in Ensenada. It's a place where all the American fugitives hang out. It's down by the ocean. The last time I spoke with LaMonica he told me that's where I could find him. He floats back and forth across the border, but he uses phony I.D. that he makes himself. Your only chance of catching him is down there." She combed her hair with her fingernails.

"What kind of car does LaMonica drive?" Carr said.

"All different," Rosemary Cramp said. "He rents 'em with counterfeit I.D., drives 'em for a couple of weeks, and then dumps 'em."

"Friends?"

"He's a one-hundred-percent lone wolf," she said. "Take my word for it, the only chance you have of busting him is in Ensenada. The owner of the bar is a coke dealer named Teddy Mora. He owns some property in Hollywood. All I know about him is that I once fronted him a couple of phony bonds and he never paid me for 'em." She wiped her eyes again and sniffed.

"Thanks for the tip," Carr said. "And I'll see what I can do to help."

Rosemary Cramp nodded without looking at him. She pushed her chair back and stood up.

"Just a sec," Carr said. He tilted his head in the direction of the blond deputy. "Do you know that deputy's name?" he asked.

"Betty Sanders," Rosemary Cramp said. "She was working the max unit when I did time in here a few years ago."

"Thanks again," Carr said.

Rosemary Cramp turned and shuffled to the inmates' door. She walked out of the room without looking back.

Charles Carr glanced at his wristwatch. It was almost 8:00 A.M. On his way out, he stopped at the bulletproof window. The blond deputy looked up from a pocket novel.

"How about breakfast?" Carr said.

"Not unless you can remember my name."

"Betty Sanders, how could I forget!"

Betty Sanders smiled. "We'll have breakfast at my place." She pulled a ballpoint pen from the flap pocket above her badge and wrote something on a notepad. She tore the page off the pad and shoved it through a slot below the window. Carr saw that it was an address in Highland Park. "I wouldn't expect you to still have my address. You probably threw it away. Cops always throw ladies' addresses away." She looked at her watch. "See you there in an hour." She made another mock kiss.

Carr gave a little wave. He found his way through the jail courtyard and a guard allowed him to exit the front gate. At a bank of pay telephones in the corner of the parking lot, he dropped in a dime and dialed.

"Homicide, Higgins."

"Charles Carr . . . A cutting in Hollywood last night . . . the suspect was booked for attempted murder under the name Rosanna DuMaurier . . ." Carr spelled the name. "She's working for me. I need the beef dropped to assault with a deadly weapon. Can you help?"

"I'll see what I can do," Higgins said. He spelled the name back.

"Appreciate it," Carr said and hung up.

• • •

146

The house was an older stucco construction with a red-tiled roof and arched doors and windows; one of the handful of two- and three-bedroom architectural designs that had multiplied, amoebalike, across Southern California to form its chaotic suburbia.

Carr knocked and the door swung open. Betty Sanders, wearing fresh lipstick, makeup, and a pink jogging suit, stood in front of him holding a spatula. She pinched him on the cheek and trotted back into the kitchen. "I hope you're hungry," she said. Carr closed the door. He strolled across a living room decorated with oversized pillows and stereo equipment.

"I've been married to three cops," she said. "They had three very different personalities, but the one thing they had in common was that they were all hungry twenty-four hours a day. My first husband used to eat a whole loaf of French bread with peanut butter and jelly just for a snack. He would gain weight, then stop eating for a month to trim down. Crazy."

Carr wandered into the kitchen. He removed his coat and hung it on the back of a chair. He sat down while Betty Sanders mixed strong Bloody Marys. She handed him one and they clinked glasses. Then she returned to the stove. He sipped and felt the vodka's warmth travel from throat to stomach. He closed his eyes for a moment. Had the headache gone away?

"When I gave you my number I knew you'd never call," she said. "I can always tell. If a guy puts the number in his shirt pocket, he'll never call. If he puts it in his wallet, there's a fifty-fifty chance." She flipped bacon and turned toward him. "May I ask you a question?"

Carr sipped again. He nodded.

"What do you think of me?"

"What do you mean by that?" he said, trying not to sound flippant.

"As a person," she said. "What do you think of me as a person?"

Carr stood up and took another drink. Having set the glass down, he stepped to the stove and turned off the burner. He took the spatula out of Betty Sanders's hand and dropped it on the counter. He kissed her. She threw her arms around him. After a while, their mouths parted.

"You can't answer that question, can you?" she whispered.

His hand reached for her crotch. She closed her eyes. Her hips moved to him. They kissed again. They held hands on the way to the bedroom. Sitting on the bed, they stripped off each other's clothes.

"I want you to shower with me first," she said. He got undressed and followed her to the bathroom. They showered and rushed back to the bed. Without drying off, they made love. Betty Sanders's love-moans seemed to get louder and louder. As she reached her height of passion, it occurred to Carr that the neighbors might call the police to report a screaming woman. Finally, they were spent. At her insistence, they showered again. As Betty Sanders pulled on her jogging suit, she said, "I like you. I really mean that."

Carr yanked on his trousers. "I like you too," he said.

"No you don't," she said. After a couple of brush strokes through her hair, she hurried back to the kitchen.

As Carr finished dressing, he heard the sound of eggs frying. He combed his hair.

The phone rang and Betty Sanders picked up the kitchen extension. "I'm really tied up at the moment, Bob," she said without attempting to lower her voice. "Try me tomorrow." Kiss sounds.

Carr joined her in the kitchen and they shared breakfast. During the meal, they discussed the possible deputy sheriffs' strike until they began to repeat themselves in agreeing with one another. They lit cigarettes. Carr looked at his watch.

"I know," she said. "It's time for you to get back to work."

The telephone rang. She answered it. "Sorry, John, but I'm kind of busy today. Try me day after tomorrow." More kisses into the receiver.

Carr stood up to leave and she led him to the door. They kissed. "Thanks for the breakfast," Carr said.

"You're a very sneaky person," she said. "After you left the jail, that prisoner told me you asked her my name."

Carr smiled. "I confess."

She opened the door for him. He stepped out. "I'll call you sometime," he said.

"Sure."

CHAPTER 19

Carr stepped into Norbert Waeves's office. Waeves was sitting behind an oversized desk covered with disassembled pipes, tobacco-stained rags, and pipe cleaners. Without looking up, Waeves scraped tobacco sludge off a pipe stem and wiped it neatly on the corner of a rag.

"You wanted to see me?" Carr said.

"Sit down," Waeves said without looking up.

Carr remained standing.

"Tell me about your proposed trip to Ensenada," Waeves said in the tone of a grade-school teacher.

"I have a couple of leads on LaMonica," Carr said. "I need to check some things out down there."

"I take it you're aware that the operations manual requires headquarters' approval for any investigation outside the continental limits of the United States," Waeves said. He still hadn't looked up. He took a penknife and dug into a pipe bowl shaped like a man's head.

"The manual also gives the agent in charge the authority to send agents out of the U.S. on any case he designates as a priority investigation," Carr said.

"The word *priority* has different meanings to different people," Waeves said.

"I'm sure headquarters will approve the trip," Carr said. "LaMonica is a federal fugitive. He murdered one of our informants."

Waeves rapped the pipe on an ashtray. "Headquarters requires an operations plan for such trips."

"I'm not asking to go to Mongolia. Ensenada is a two-and-a-half-hour drive from Los Angeles. I'm told that the police there are cooperative."

Waeves lifted a pipe stem to his lips and blew. Using a corner of a rag, he dabbed at the device and then examined the stain on the rag. "For the time being I'm going to disapprove the trip," he said.

"Why?" Carr asked angrily.

Waeves looked at him disdainfully. "I'm going to deny travel permission because it sounds to me like you're going off . . . uh . . . half-cocked, shall we say?"

Carr turned and walked out of the room. He returned to his office and fell into his desk chair.

Kelly was writing a report. He put down his pen. "What did he want?" he said.

"He refused to let us go below the border," Carr said, looking at the wall.

"Let me guess," Kelly said, holding an arm out in traffic-cop fashion. "He quoted the manual, right?"

"Right."

"Which means, *one,* that he doesn't want to go to the trouble of writing an operations plan; and *two,* he won't deem the case a priority. That figures. He doesn't know how to write an operations plan because he got his promotions by kissing ass in D.C. while he was an instructor in Agent Training School. He probably wouldn't recognize an operations plan if one jumped up and bit him. As far as deeming the case a priority investigation, *no way.* That would mean taking a stand on something, choosing one way or the other. Therefore, what you see is what you always get. *No waves.*"

Carr picked up a partially completed form titled "Request to Use Government-Owned Vehicle for More Than One Calendar Day" off his desk. He tore it in half and tossed it into the wastebasket.

Kelly's face turned red. "Of all the briefcase-carrying, useless-as-tits-on-a-bull bureaucrats living on the face of the planet Earth, No Waves is the worst. I really believe that. One minute after I retire I'm going to walk right into his office and sock him in the goddamn mouth. I'm going to knock every one of his teeth out." He slammed fist into palm.

Carr got up from his desk and walked to the window. It was rush hour. Buses and cars were lined up at entrances to freeways. People couldn't wait to get out of the city.

It was daybreak.

Jack Kelly sat at a tiny table next to the kitchen window and finished off his usual three eggs and six slices of bacon. He was dressed in Levi's, boots and a flannel shirt.

The first rays of sun glistened off the dew collected on the sides of an olive-drab pup tent pitched in the backyard. Next to the tent, an L.A. Rams pennant topped a broomstick flagpole.

"The boys didn't get to sleep out there till midnight," Rose Kelly said. "They were roughhousing."

Kelly chuckled.

"Will you be back for late Mass on Sunday?" Rose said, speaking to the stove. Her long red braid twitched back and forth on her shoulders as she labored. She wore a housecoat. Rose Kelly was the kind of woman who would not allow her husband to leave the house without eating. Perhaps for this attribute alone, Jack Kelly would have chosen her for a wife.

"I'll sure try," he said.

Rose Kelly refilled his cup from a steaming coffeepot, then sat down at the table. "You haven't been fishing in years," she said.

"Spur-of-the-moment idea," Kelly said, staring into his cup. His hand drummed fingers.

"Just you and Charlie Carr?"

"Uh, right," Kelly said.

"Isn't Mexico kind of a long way to go for fishing?"

A horn honked. Kelly jumped up. He pulled a baseball cap out of his back pocket and pulled it on. Rose stood up, kissed him on the lips, and gave him a hug. "I know it has something to do with your job," she said apologetically as she nuzzled his neck.

"God bless you, Rose," Kelly said.

She followed him to the front door. Outside, Carr sat behind the wheel of his sedan. Fishing poles protruded from a rear window.

"Please be careful," Rose Kelly said as her husband walked out the door and down the driveway.

LaMonica dropped pesos into a pay phone hanging on a wall next to the hotel's reception desk. He told the operator to make the call collect from Roger Brown. After a minute or two, Omar T. Lockhart clicked onto the line.

"Have you considered my client's offer?" LaMonica said.

"Yes, we have," Lockhart said.

There was a silence.

"Are we going to be able to go any further?" LaMonica said. He held his breath.

"I have been authorized to meet with you once more," Lockhart said. "I'd prefer to have the meeting here in Houston."

"Sorry," LaMonica said. "You'll have to come back down here. My client demands this." Another silence.

"Very well," Lockhart said, sounding angry.

It was siesta time. LaMonica and Lockhart sat at one of the poolside umbrella tables, Sandy between them. A sun-burned young woman in her early twenties splashed around in the shallow end of the greenish pool with a man of the same age. They swam away from and then toward one another lazily, like goldfish in a bowl.

Lockhart had neither smiled nor so much as touched the ~~margarita sitting in front of~~ him during the entire hour or so of half-whispered, half-spoken negotiations.

"Fifty thousand is my last offer," Lockhart said. "It's a company decision and it's final. I have been authorized to tell you that you can take it or leave it." Rivulets of perspiration extended from the fat man's sideburns to his jawline.

"I'll take it," Sandy said. "But I'm getting screwed and it's just not right." Haughtily, she folded her arms across her chest.

The fat man dug a handkerchief out of his back pocket and unfolded it. Covering his face with the cloth, he wiped from side to side. He looked at the hanky and stuffed it back into his pocket. "My employer insists that the transfer itself take place in the United States."

With eyes closed, Sandy shook her head. "No way," she said.

"We're not going to negotiate on this point," Lockhart said, "because I'm sure you don't *really* expect us to bring fifty thousand dollars in cold cash across the border." He stood up and straightened his wrinkled trousers.

"You will if you want the checks," Sandy said.

"No, young lady, we damn well *won't*," Lockhart said. "Texans don't do business that way. You'll come to the U.S. to do the final deal or it will not be done at all." His eyes bugged with hostility.

LaMonica's hands made a "go easy" gesture and he winked at the security man.

"I'll expect to hear from you soon," said Lockhart. He turned and trudged along the edge of the pool and through the hotel lobby.

"I'm not going across," Sandy said. "I told you I wouldn't go and I wasn't bullshitting. I have the creeps just being here in T-Town. You've heard the stories about the feds kidnapping fugitives and driving them across. I'm not going to take a chance on going back to eating off a plastic tray and sitting in a room with fifty bull dykes just to watch a television program."

LaMonica leaned closer to her. "You're not looking at this realistically," he said. "These people are ready to *pay*. You and I will get twenty-five thousand fucking dollars apiece! We will be *out* of this shitty border scene. I'm talking about *freedom*, Sandy. A ticket *out*."

Sandy's fingernails played a tune on her lower lip.

"I'll be with you every step of the way," LaMonica said confidently. "We can pull it off without any problems. I know we can."

"I've heard that before," Sandy said. "Besides, you don't give a shit about me or any other woman. For you, women are just something to use."

"We're *both* going to be there. We're *both* wanted in the U.S. I'm not asking you to take any risk I'm not taking. In fact, if something happens I'll let you hand me up. I'm giving you my permission to tell the cops I forced you into the operation against your will. You can cut a deal and testify against me. I'm giving you my permission to do that if anything happens. I swear."

"Deal or not, I've still got an escape warrant that would put me back in the joint," Sandy Hartzbecker said. *"That's what it all comes down to."*

LaMonica grabbed her arm. "No," he said, speaking through gritted teeth. "What it all comes down to is that fat motherfucker Lockhart sitting across the border with fifty grand wrapped in rubber bands and whether we go over and take him off or just sit here and listen to one another talk about it. I'll tell you this much: With or without your help, I'm going to go up there and *try* to take the man's money. I'll hold a gun to his head if I have to."

Sandy pulled her arm away. She stood up and faced the pool. She watched the two human dolphins as they continued to splash around. It was a long while before she spoke.

"I want Mr. Cool to be there with me," she said. "That way I know I won't get ripped off."

LaMonica grimaced. "Involving other people in our business is suicide. It's unnecessary."

"It's the only way I'll do it. I mean that."

LaMonica sat for a while without speaking. "Okay," he said finally. "You're risking as much as I am by letting him in on it. Go ahead and call him. Tell him we'll do the deal at the Sandstone Motor Lodge on Interstate Five just south of San Diego. He should get a room there day after tomorrow and wait for us."

CHAPTER 20

They were less than a hundred feet from the border, waiting in a line of automobiles.

LaMonica's mouth and throat seemed to become drier and drier as they approached the international boundary. His mind was on the sleeping bag in the trunk that contained the phony traveler's checks. He wore a straw sombrero with the word *Mexico* stitched across the brim.

Sandy squirmed in the passenger seat. "I should have walked across," she said out of the side of her mouth. "You could have picked me up on the other side."

"Too complicated," LaMonica said. He stepped on the accelerator and the car advanced. "Just relax. Look the cop in the eye," he said.

"What are you bringing into the U.S.?" the younger border patrolman said, standing at the driver's window. His olive-green uniform was starched, neat; a brass nameplate over his pocket read "C. Roberts."

LaMonica flicked the brim of his silly hat. "Just this," he said. Turning to Sandy. "And I'm afraid the wife is bringing back Montezuma's revenge." Sandy shook her head as if she were embarrassed.

The patrolman smiled. He stepped back from the car and waved them across the line.

LaMonica accelerated into the stream of traffic heading north toward San Diego. Sandy held out her hands. They were shaking. "Look at me," she said.

LaMonica flipped the sombrero onto the backseat. "That hat is worth a million bucks," he said. "It's all they look at."

Less than fifteen minutes up the road LaMonica steered onto a freeway off ramp. At the end of the ramp he turned left and followed a bridge that doubled back across the freeway. He pulled up in front of a motel, a two-story rectangular affair with a coffee shop. Having parked the car, he strolled into the registration office. The woman behind the desk was gray-haired, hefty and wore a flowered dress. Her eyeglasses hung precariously on the top of her nose. She handed LaMonica a registration card and a pen. He signed it "C. Roberts."

In the motel room, LaMonica stood at the window while Sandy relaxed in a chair. "I thought we were going to meet at the Sandstone Motel," she said with a puzzled look. "I told Mr. Cool to meet us there."

LaMonica pointed out the window. "The Sandstone is just across the freeway," he said. "Your man is already there. That looks like his Caddy parked in the lot in front of that room."

LaMonica walked to a nightstand. He picked up the phone and dialed an area code and a number.

"Teddy's Bar," Mora said.

"I need a favor," LaMonica said.

"Shoot."

"I want you to drive up toward San Diego. Stop at the Sandstone Motel Lodge on Interstate Five. There's a telephone booth next to the registration office. I'll call you on that phone. Make sure you travel clean," LaMonica said.

"Gotcha," Mora said. "Can you give me a clue as to what the hell is going down?"

"I don't like to talk on the phone," LaMonica said. "I'll tell you when you get here." He hung up.

The air was filled with the gentle thunder of waves.

Sea gulls, none of which looked the least bit overfed, made swooping attacks on edible items along the strand, then fluttered back to the grassy hillocks above it where Carr and Kelly had been hiding since morning. The birds seemed to launch themselves without urgency, as if to keep from getting bored.

It was high tide, nearing dusk, and Carr's legs felt numb and stiff. Maintaining a low-crawl position among the chaparral, the T-man and his partner faced the portion of shore that included Teddy's Bar. They were far enough away that binoculars were needed to make out the faces of those coming and going from the modest establishment but close enough so that when the wind was right, they could hear the sound of Mariachi music coming from the open front door.

Carr looked at his wristwatch, a habit he had always tried to avoid on surveillances because it seemed to make time slow down.

"We're gonna have to move in closer as soon as it gets dark," Kelly said. "If Teddy slips by we could still be up here with these sea gulls tomorrow morning. Wouldn't that be a goddamn knockout punch? Being up here all day peeing in the bushes waiting for Teddy to make a move and we *miss* him when he leaves?"

Carr smiled. "Sounds like you're not enjoying our little fishing trip."

"On the contrary!" Kelly said sarcastically. "How could I say it hasn't been just *barrels* of fun being down here in Baja dodging sea-gull shit. I've particularly enjoyed having a pound or so of sand wedged up the crack of my ass all day. Not to mention the third-degree sunburn I've developed on the back of my neck. *Golly*, I haven't had so many kicks since my double hernia."

A light-colored Mercedes sedan made a dust cloud as it came down the road. Carr grabbed the binoculars. The vehicle had California license plates and was driven by a man wearing a wide-brimmed gambler's hat. He parked the sedan in front of the bar and got out. Carr guessed him at no more then five feet tall. Having taken a quick glance around, the man proceeded to the trunk of the vehicle. He unlocked it and the lid popped up. Sticking his hand in what looked like a leather bag, he pulled out a handful of small white packets. With one smooth motion he hoisted his pants leg and shoved the items into his sock. After closing and locking the trunk, he strolled into the bar.

"So far, everyone who has gone into the place has looked one-hundred-percent *wrong*," Kelly said.

Carr put down the binoculars and rubbed his eyes. "Sure seems that way," he said.

Kelly pulled a handkerchief out of his back pocket and spread it out in his hand. Tucking one of its sides under the back of his baseball cap, he allowed the cloth to cover the back of his neck, legionnaire style. "Matter of fact, from the looks of the people so far, I'd say if you wanted to give the world an enema you could probably start by sticking the nozzle right in the front door down there," he said.

Carr grabbed the binoculars and adjusted the focus. "That's him," he said.

Teddy Mora, wearing a tropical shirt, came out of the bar. Ostrichlike, he sauntered across the parking lot and headed toward a green camper truck. Mora unlocked the driver's door and got in. The engine roared as he headed up a road leading to the highway.

The agents jumped up and ran through the chaparral like firemen heading for a hook-and-ladder. Carr vaulted into the driver's seat and started the engine. Kelly jumped in on the passenger side and slammed the door. Throwing the sedan into gear, Carr hit the accelerator and zoomed toward the highway at full speed. Nearing the main road, he caught a glimpse of Teddy Mora's camper proceeding north at what seemed a leisurely pace. The T-man steered through brush and bumped across rocks and onto the highway. Adjusting his speed, he was able to keep Mora's camper truck barely within sight. As it grew dark, Carr kept up the cat-and-mouse game by turning the sedan's brights on and off intermittently as they rounded curves.

By the time they reached the outskirts of Tijuana, it was dark. The green camper truck wound through the border town's business district, a winding maze of illuminated beer advertisements and winking neon that touted B-girl dives with names like Sailor's Lounge, Rosa's and Hula Girl. At the western edge of the town, the camper made a turn and followed a sign pointing toward the U.S. The vehicle crossed a small bridge and pulled into one of the lines of cars inching up to the border.

"He's going across," Kelly said. "Should we stay on him?"

"We might as well see where he's going," Carr said.

"With our luck, he's probably going across the line to pick up a six-pack of American beer," Kelly said.

At the checkpoint, a border patrolman leaned down and said something to Mora. Mora answered. The patrolman stepped back from the camper. He nodded, and Mora drove into the United States.

Carr followed, using other vehicles on the freeway for cover. He sped up as they neared the outskirts of San Diego. Maneuvering the sedan around some vehicles, he pulled up to within three car-lengths of the green camper. "We'd better stay close," Kelly said. "He might turn off for town."

"That's not it," Carr said in a worried tone. "I think it's the wrong camper."

"You're right," Kelly said angrily.

Stepping on the gas, Carr zoomed past the vehicle. Ahead on the highway were a couple of sports cars and a sedan pulling a boat.

"Sheey*it!*" Kelly said. "He must have already turned off. *We missed him!*"

Carr jammed the accelerator to the floor. The car sped north on the highway for two miles. Teddy's camper was nowhere in sight.

"Time to backtrack," Carr said.

Carr swung the sedan violently onto the dirt shoulder of

the road, threw a wheel-spinning U-turn, and crashed across the curb and grass in the middle of the highway. Racing south, he took the next off ramp. Similarly structured motels had been built on either side of the freeway. Slowing down, Carr pulled into the nearest motel parking lot. He drove slowly, scrutinizing the rows of automobiles. It took a few minutes to cover the whole lot.

"Sheeyit!" Kelly said. "We've lost him. We came all the way to Mexico on our day off and lost him!" The Irishman's bear-paw hands slammed the dashboard. "*Shee-hee-yit!*"

"Let's check out the motel on the other side of the freeway," Carr said.

He maneuvered the sedan up the street and into another motel lot.

The green camper was parked under a strong streetlight next to the motel office. "There's our boy," Carr said. "Standing by that phone booth."

"Must be some kind of a deal," Kelly said.

Carr's eyes surveyed the other cars parked in the lot. He made one pass and drove out of the lot and up a grade that led to a residential area. They passed a foreign car facing down the hill toward the motel. It was occupied by two young men.

"Looks like Teddy might be in a little trouble," Carr said.

Kelly nodded. "Now that you mention it, there were some people sitting in cars . . ."

Carr pulled into a parking space across from a Spanish stucco home. Below, the motel parking lot was in full view. Teddy paced around the telephone booth. He kept looking at his watch.

"This could be real interesting," Kelly said.

LaMonica had been staring out the motel window for a long while.

Sandy stood in front of the bathroom mirror applying makeup. "I'm going to go over there and talk to Mr. Cool," she said.

"Not just yet," LaMonica said, leaning against the window frame. "I want to show you something."

She came to the window and stood beside him. "Just watch for a few minutes," he said.

She gave him a puzzled look. "What am I supposed to be watching for?" she said. "Oh, there's Teddy's camper."

LaMonica grabbed the phone off the table beside him and dialed.

A woman's voice: "Sandstone Motel."

"Mr. Cole's room, please," LaMonica said.

The phone clicked. Mr. Cool said hello.

"This is LaMonica. Sandy wanted me to phone you. We've decided to call the thing off. I just spoke with Teddy. He says there's cops watching the Sandstone. He's got the package in his camper right now—the whole thing. I told him to get his ass back across the border as fast as possible. You'd better do the same." LaMonica set the receiver down. He picked it up again and dialed.

Sandy stared at him. "Why did you tell him there was something wrong? Why did you lie to him?" she said angrily.

"Keep your eyes on Teddy," he said. LaMonica dialed the pay booth. The phone rang.

"Teddy's going into the phone booth," she said.

"Hello." It was Teddy's voice.

"The whole thing is burned!" LaMonica said. "Get the hell out of there right now! We've been snitched off. Cops all over the place!" He slammed the phone down.

Teddy ran out of the booth to the camper truck. Men in street clothes jumped out of vehicles and ran to the camper. They had guns. Cars sped into the motel lot.

"Cops!" Sandy said.

The plainclothes cops spread-eagled Teddy against the side of his camper truck. They ripped seats and bedding out of the van and tossed it on the pavement. Teddy was searched and searched again.

Sandy shook her head for a long while. Finally she dropped back on the bed as if she had been punched in the stomach. "It had to be Mr. Cool," she said stoically. "Mr.

Cool is an informant." Her hands covered her face. "That rotten . . . How did you know?" she moaned.

"Just an educated guess," LaMonica said.

"What about Teddy?" she said.

"They've got nothing on him," LaMonica said. "They'll have to let him go." He picked up the telephone.

"Who are you going to call now?" Sandy muttered.

"Lockhart," he said. "Now it's safe to go ahead with our thing."

CHAPTER 21

Kelly used the binoculars to get a better view of the activity at the Sandstone Motel. "Feebs," he said. He put the binoculars in Carr's hands. "That's my guess."

Carr used the binoculars for a moment. "You pegged that one," he said. "Tom Luegner just walked out of one of the rooms."

"I wonder what that asshole is doing down here?" Kelly said.

Plainclothesmen climbed in and out of Teddy's camper. They took out the seats and put them back. Someone lifted the hood of the vehicle and fiddled around in the engine compartment. The hubcaps were removed and replaced. Luegner pointed his finger at Teddy's face. The gaunt man kept throwing his hands up and gesturing at his van. Other agents milled about. Some made notes on clipboards. The camper was searched again. Finally, after an hour or so, Teddy was allowed to leave. He got in his truck and drove out of the lot, steering south when he reached the freeway.

The FBI men took their time piling into vehicles and departing. Only Luegner was left. After a while, the crowd of motel guests that had gathered to watch the gangbusters returned to their rooms.

A black man came out of a ground-floor room. He approached Luegner sheepishly, shaking his head. As he spoke, he kept throwing up his hands.

"He must be the snitch," Kelly said.

Carr nodded. "Could be," he said.

Luegner patted the man on the shoulder. The black man shook his head some more and returned to his room. Luegner climbed into his sedan and departed. Minutes later the black man exited his room and climbed into a gold Cadillac. Carr noted the personalized license plate: MR COOL.

"Let's follow him," Carr said.

"What for?" his partner said.

"It might be interesting."

Carr started the engine. He drove down the hill and waited near the freeway. The Cadillac headed south. The agents followed, keeping far behind. When it became clear that they were about to cross the border again, Kelly made a gruff remark about having nothing better to do on a weekend than drive in and out of Mexico.

They followed the Cadillac through Tijuana and along the coast past Rosarita Beach. By the time they reached Ensenada it was almost midnight. The black man pulled into a motel at the edge of town and parked. He climbed out of the Cadillac and strolled to a room near the swimming pool. Removing a key from his pocket, he unlocked the door and went in.

Carr and Kelly approached the motel room carefully. The light was still on. Carr put his ear to the door. Out of the corner of his eye he saw Kelly slip his revolver out of its holster and hold it in the pocket of his windbreaker. They positioned themselves on either side of the door. There was the sound of a radio playing rock music.

Carr knocked. The sound of a drawer being opened and closed. "Who's there?" said the black man.

"Agent Carr. My partner and I work with Tom Luegner." He kept his voice low. Footsteps came to the door. Carr thought he could hear the man breathing.

"What do you want?"

"Tom asked us to run something by ya," Carr said.

Nothing was said for a few moments, and then, "Slide your I.D. card under the door."

"Sure." Carr removed his Treasury credential from his wallet and shoved it under the door.

"This ain't no Bureau I.D.," said the voice inside.

"Look man, Tom Luegner and I work together on a federal agency task force," Carr said. "You can call him if you want," he said, showing a set of crossed fingers to Kelly.

Footsteps. A drawer was pulled open and something heavy was tossed inside. The drawer slammed closed. Moments later, the chain latch was removed and the black man pulled open the door. Without a greeting, he shuffled to a chair and plopped down.

"What is all this bullshit, man? I need to get me some muthafuckin' sleep."

"Sorry to wake you up," Carr said, "but Tom said you wouldn't mind talking with us for a few minutes. It's about LaMonica."

The black man rubbed his eyes. "I don't know nothin' about the muthafucka 'cept he's a paper man and he escaped from the federal joint. He's got a crib down here, but nobody knows exactly where it is. Say, how come Tom isn't asking me these muthafuckin' questions his *own* self? He knows I don't like to be meetin' a lot of muthafuckin' people."

"What kind of paper is LaMonica into right now?" Carr said. He sat down on the edge of the bed.

"Fuck if I know. I didn't even know what kind of muthafuckin' paper was supposed to be delivered at the Sandstone tonight. I just knew the thing was supposed to go down there. I worked my way in through this bitch ya see. She's LaMonica's ex-girl friend. She's using me as insurance cuz she don't trust the muthafucka." The black man's eyes were on Kelly. The Irishman stood at the dresser staring at a flipped-open wallet. "Luegner told me he wasn't going to give my identity to anyone else. He told me I didn't have to meet no other cops." The man's eyes darted back and forth between the T-men. "I don't think I'd better say anything else until I talk with him."

Carr smiled. "Tom Luegner is my brother-in-law. I helped him get hired at the Bureau. We do favors for one another. Is that too hard to understand?"

"How do I know that?"

"We were at the Sandstone tonight." Carr smiled amusedly.

"Then why didn't Tom introduce me to you?"

"We were on a surveillance post up on a hill," Kelly said.

The black man shook his head. "Somehow that muthafuckin' LaMonica smelled a muthafuckin' rat," he said. "The package was close by. The whole million in checks had to be close by. I told Tom that. I would have bet my muthafuckin' ass on it."

"What kind of checks?" Carr said.

The black man's expression changed to one of fear. His eyes were suddenly on a dresser drawer. "Didn't Tom tell you I didn't know what kind of checks?"

Carr shook his head.

"I don't think I'd better say anything else until I talk with Tom." The black man said this in the hesitant tone of someone who had dialed the wrong number.

Kelly stood at the door. He reached behind him and opened it with his left hand. The agents walked out to the sedan. Kelly was mumbling under his breath. Inside the car he took out a pen and notebook and scribbled. "I got a name and number off a driver's license," he said.

"Ten to one he's wanted," Carr said.

Kelly laughed. "I'd say he didn't exactly look like your average Baja tourist."

The Ensenada police station was a diminutive green building that reminded Carr of the tiny one- and two-bedroom stucco homes that dotted the narrow streets in East Los Angeles where he'd grown up.

Kelly followed him in the front door. The place contained an office with three desks and a steel door that probably led to the prisoner lockup. The walls looked like the walls of any police station: lots of photographs and sketches of ugly people, lists of names, duty rosters. In the corner was a gun rack that contained a shiny Thompson submachine gun.

A stocky Mexican man wearing a rumpled black suit with a Mexican flag lapel pin and a snap-brim hat was parked behind a desk. He held a peeled orange like a hand grenade. Deftly, he slid his roller chair to a wastebasket and leaned over. Without so much as acknowledging the Americans' presence, the barrel-chested cop bit viciously into the orange. The juice from the fruit dripped into the basket. With two or three chomps, wet and loud, the fruit disappeared. Using two fingers, the Mexican pulled a handkerchief from his back pocket and wiped his mouth thoroughly, taking special care to dab his Pancho Villa mustache. He wiped his hands on the rag and put it away.

"Do you speak English?" Kelly said.

"If I didn't, I guess you'd be shit out of luck," the cop said. He rolled back behind his desk.

The T-men looked at one another. Carr thought the cop's shirt looked like it would pop its buttons. The desk plate read "A. Rodriguez—Chief of Detectives."

"L.A. cops on vacation, right?" Rodriguez said.

"U.S. Treasury agents," Carr said. He showed his gold badge.

"Federales," Rodriguez said sarcastically.

"We're looking for an American fugitive," Carr said. He handed Rodriguez a mug shot of Paul LaMonica. "He hangs around Teddy's Bar."

The policeman examined the photograph with a blank expression. "All the American assholes hang around Teddy's Bar," he said offhandedly. He tossed the photo on the desk.

"Does the face ring a bell?" Carr asked.

"I've seen him around," Rodriguez said. He opened a desk drawer and pulled out another orange.

"Do you know where he lives?" Kelly said.

"I can find out." Rodriguez bit a hole in the orange and pulled off large chunks of peel. "And just what are you gonna do if I find him?"

Carr and Kelly looked at one another.

"This ain't your ranch down here, cowboys," Rodriguez said before they could answer. "If you take someone into custody in Mexico, it's kidnapping. You arrest them, then I arrest you. How would you like that, eh, cowboys?" He rolled over to the basket, still chomping the orange. More juice.

Carr stared at the Mexican. "He's a federal prison escapee and he killed one of my informants," Carr said.

The cop went through his wipe-off routine again, then stood up. Carr figured his height at more than six-foot-two. "And what would you tell me if I came across the border into your country and said I was looking for some sonofabitch? Huh? What would you tell me?" Rodriguez's eyes were half shut.

"We'd probably tell you that *we'd* handle it," Carr said.

"That's right, cowboys. And that's what I'm telling you. *I'll* handle it . . . by the proper police procedures."

Kelly's face was red. "And what does that mean?" he said.

"That means when I find the sonofabitch you're looking for, I kick his ass, handcuff him, toss him in the backseat of my car and drive him up to the border where you people are waiting. I pull the sonofabitch out of the car and boot his ass across the line to you. That way things are done nice and legal." The detective smiled broadly. His canine teeth were gold.

The special agents smiled back. Carr introduced himself. He shook hands, as did Kelly. "Frank Garcia said to say hello," Carr said.

"You're friends with Frank?" The Mexican's eyes lit up.

Carr nodded. "Drinking buddies."

The Mexican laughed loudly. He picked up the mug

shot. "In that case, maybe we'll kill this *pendejo* when we catch him. You just say the word."

"Thanks anyway," Carr said. He smiled wanly.

"But first we've got to catch the sonofabitch." Rodriguez picked up the phone and dialed. "There's only one real-estate man in town who rents to Americans." He held a phone conversation in Spanish. Near the end of the conversation he wrote something down. He said *gracias* and hung up. "This *pendejo* used the name Roger Brown when he rented the place . . . paid two months' rent in advance." Rodriguez stood and pulled a cowboy-style two-gun belt out of a desk drawer. He fastened it around his waist. "Let's go, men." He yanked the submachine gun from its rack and strode out the door.

The patrol car sped south along the coast. Rodriguez had turned on the red light and siren as if they were heading for a bank robbery in progress. He rounded turns in the narrow road like a stock-car racer. A few miles south of town the detective vaulted the police car off the pavement and onto a dirt road. Kicking up a camouflage of dirt, he raced along a path bounded by heavy chaparral and fir trees for a few miles. Finally, at a clearing, the vehicle was brought to a halt. The siren was turned off. Ahead of them, at the edge of the woods, lay the charred remains of a small structure. It was surrounded by a makeshift fence that the fire had not touched. The men exited the vehicle and stared at the ruins, the dust from the police car swirling around them like smoke.

"The *pendejo* sure as hell doesn't live here anymore," Rodriguez said.

Kicking through the debris, Carr made his way into the middle of the charred pile. He picked up a half-burnt scrap of lumber and poked at the ashes. "LaMonica is a counterfeiter," Carr said without looking up. "He may have had a good reason to burn this place down."

The Mexican detective furrowed his brow. *"Destroying the evidence,"* he said somberly. He turned on his heel and headed back to the patrol car. Having unlocked the vehicle's trunk, he flung it open. He pulled out a shovel and a pick and tossed them on the ground. Without hesitation, he removed his coat and unfastened his gun belt. He dropped them in the trunk. Stripping off his dress shirt, he hung it neatly from the trunk latch. He grabbed the tools and strutted into the middle of the ashes like a bull entering a ring. He tossed the shovel at the T-men and went to work with the pick.

CHAPTER 22

By noon it was a hundred degrees. The three men were covered with soot and perspiration. Rodriguez had made a beer run for which he refused to accept any money; there was a pile of Carta Blanca bottles in the trunk of the squad car.

Kelly stood to the rear of the ash pile. He poked the point of a handkerchief into his eye for a moment and pulled it out. He wiped something on the back of his hand. "Got it," he said. "It felt like I had a two-by-four stuck in there."

Carr kept digging, hacking around.

Next to the patrol car lay a collection of items that had withstood the fire: a couple of ink cans (labels burned off), a feeder that looked like it might have come off a printing press, a charred paper cutter . . .

Rodriguez was fifty or so yards away in a clump of trees. He whistled. The T-men sauntered over. The Mexican pointed to the ground between some trees where the earth appeared freshly spaded. Without a word the men began digging. The sound of metal on metal. Carr dropped to his knees and dug with his hands. "It's a printing press," he said.

They took turns digging. Finally the upper section of the machine was free. Following Rodriguez's suggestion, they used a rope to attach the press to the rear bumper of the police car. The Mexican started the engine and pulled the press, dirt and all, from its burial site. Oddly, it came out of the groud upright, as if all the machine needed was a brushing off to be operable again. The men used bare hands to knock the remaining dirt off the moving parts. "There's no blanket roller," Kelly said.

The cop looked puzzled.

"The blanket roller might have an ink impression of what was printed," Carr explained.

Rodriguez nodded. He stepped closer to the heavy machine. As if the machine were an adversary, he slammed his open palms against it. With a mighty shove, he knocked the printing press over. With another flurry of hands, the men cleared the dirt off the bottom of the press. A piece of white bond paper was stuck to the base of the apparatus. Carr pulled it off. There was nothing on it except a glob of purple ink. They passed the sheet around.

"The inks that LaMonica bought in L.A.," Kelly said. "Blue and red . . ."

"Makes purple," Carr said. "Blue and red makes purple."

"But what the hell kind of negotiable paper is printed with purple ink?" Kelly scratched his head. "Foreign money maybe, or checks."

"Could be any number of things," Carr said.

"It's for sure the sonofabitch didn't go to all this trouble to cover up printing birthday paper," Rodriguez said. He laughed loudly.

It wasn't yet noon, which probably accounted for the fact that the motel bar was nearly empty. LaMonica faced Lockhart across a cocktail table hidden in a corner. Other than the whispers of the two men, the only sound in the place was the splashing of highball glasses as the bartender dunked them in and out of soapy water.

"I want to see your money," LaMonica said. "Surely you

don't expect me to just hand over the package of checks and hope for the best. Like what's to stop you from taking the checks and just flat out *walking away?* You're smart enough to know my client can't stroll into the local police station and make a complaint about someone stealing her phony checks." Staring at the fat man, he swished the ice in his drink and took a sip.

Lockhart finished his drink and looked into the glass. "On the other hand," he said, "you see no danger in me showing you people fifty thousand dollars—*real dollars,* mind you, not some worthless printed paper shit like you are selling, but real honest-to-God *greenbacks.*" He shook his head. "You must think I'm a rube, Mr. Brown, an honest-to-Christ, shit-shoveling hillbilly."

LaMonica's finger pointed at the other man's chest. "On the contrary," he said. "You're like a lot of executive types. Always holding a few cards out of the deck. And as a matter of fact, you're holding one right this very minute."

"And what might that be?" Lockhart said, leaning back in his chair.

"The goon you had with you at the Houston Airport. He's your man. He followed me. Do you want to sit there and deny that?" LaMonica smiled sardonically.

The fat man's face reddened. He fidgeted.

"Don't embarrass yourself by saying no," LaMonica said. "Now, if you are so pure and honest, then why have a goon to follow me? Why the muscle? I'll tell you why . . . because you're planning to *rip us off*. It would probably mean a promotion for you. Maybe even a fucking double Christmas bonus! Recover the checks without spending a dime out of the good old company till. I know how you people think and so does my client."

"You really are paranoid, aren't you?" the fat man said. There was a mist of perspiration on his brow.

"I don't like the way you do business," LaMonica said.

The men stared at one another for a while.

"We're not going to get anywhere like this," said the security man. "I came here to discuss the final transfer. You keep changing the subject."

"There's nothing more to discuss," LaMonica said. "You can show me your money or the whole deal is off."

"Then the goddamn deal is off," Lockhart said. He stood up abruptly. "If you change your mind and choose to do it my way, I'll be in my room for the next thirty minutes. And don't try to contact me again once I leave." He marched out of the bar.

LaMonica hurried upstairs to his room. He knocked. Sandy let him in. She was dressed only in bra and panties. He rushed past her to the dresser and poured a drink. He sipped. "It's going perfectly," he said. "We're over the hump."

"What if he walks over here right now and kicks in the door? How do we know he's not secretly working with the cops? He's got to figure that the checks are right here in the room."

LaMonica slugged down the drink. "He'll have figured wrong, that's all. The checks aren't here. If he puts a gun to my head, I'll tell him that the checks are still in Mexico. He would never have the balls to drive us over the border to get them. He, and any cops, would have to walk away . . . leave us alone and walk away." He glared at her. "Why don't you put some clothes on?"

She ignored him. "What about the car? The checks are sitting right there in the trunk."

"We got here before he did," LaMonica said to the mirror. "We haven't been near the car. The parking lot is full." He looked at his watch. "Things are going perfectly."

"I'm keyed up," Sandy said. She fingered the elastic band on her panties. "If you feel like it, so do I. I want to get my mind off this whole thing for a few minutes."

LaMonica's mind was still on the details as he unzipped his trousers.

Lockhart sat at the tiny desk in his motel room, the phone to his ear. He wore a .38 in a shoulder holster. The rig caused his armpits to perspire more than usual. Next to the telephone was a box of doughnuts with three jellyfilleds left. He knew that such between-meal snacks were unhealthy, but at least he wasn't a heavy smoker or drinker. Someday he hoped he would be able to put his mind to the task of losing weight, but for the time being it was impossible. When he felt tense he liked to eat, and that was that.

The chairman came on the line.

"I've made my final demand, sir," Lockhart said. "I gave him an ultimatum. He is still adamant about wanting to see our money, but I don't think we should do this. It's just too dangerous under the circumstances. Is that your thinking as well, sir?"

There was a long silence. "If the checks are *there*, I want them. I want you to do what you have to do to get them."

"Well . . . uh . . . sir, do you think I should show him the money?" Lockhart said. "Just let him see it?"

"That's not what I said, Omar. I said that if the checks are there, I *want* them." The chairman enunciated each word.

"Certainly, sir," Lockhart said. He cleared his throat. "I'm on top of it. I'll make it work." *Be assertive*, he remembered from a recent one-day seminar.

"I'll wait to hear from you," the chairman said coolly. The phone clicked.

Lockhart wished there was someone with him, someone to talk the situation over with. His stomach growled. A doughnut was at his lips. He bit down and the jelly squirted pleasantly onto the corners of his mouth. He chewed. It was gone in three bites. Now there were only two left in the box. He wiped his mouth with a Kleenex. Standing up, he peeked out the curtain. "I can take care of myself," he said as if speaking to his mother.

The phone rang. Lockhart jumped backward. He took a deep breath and picked up the receiver.

"I'm willing to compromise," Roger Brown said. "We can both show at the same time. You bring yours and we bring ours and we deal. This way will be fair to both parties."

Lockhart agreed. After putting down the phone, he finished off the last two doughnuts and washed his hands thoroughly.

The motel parking lot was fairly busy: a family loading luggage into a station wagon, people coming and going from the registration office. LaMonica got in the driver's side of the rented sedan and unlocked the passenger door for Sandy. He removed a snub-nosed revolver from the glove compartment and laid it on the seat between them.

He handed Sandy a key. "Put it in your shoe," he said. "If something goes wrong and he gets the drop on us, tell him we never had the checks, that the whole thing was just a con game."

Sandy hid the key in one of her flats. "I think I have to go to the bathroom," she said.

"Nerves," he said.

"There are too many people around here," she said.

"All the safer," LaMonica said. "He'll be less likely to try anything in a public place."

Lockhart came out of the motel office carrying a briefcase. He looked around nervously and started walking toward them. There was a bulge under his left arm.

"He's packing," LaMonica said. Sandy bit her lip.

Cautiously the fat man shuffled up to the passenger window. He was out of breath. "Are you ready?" he said.

"Yes," Sandy said, "just show us that you have it."

"We agreed to do this at exactly the same time," Lockhart said.

"I have the traveler's checks," she said. "Just flash your money and let's get this thing over with. Please."

The fat man's eyes twitched. He looked around the lot again.

LaMonica's right hand gripped the butt of the revolver.

Lockhart balanced the briefcase on one hand in front of the passenger window. He flipped it open. It was filled with stacks of twenty-dollar bills. He slammed it shut again. His hand reached inside his coat. "You've seen the money. Now let's see the checks, *right now.* You'd better not try anything. I've got a gun." Lockhart's lips had turned white.

LaMonica tapped Sandy Hartzbecker's arm. She opened the passenger door and went to the trunk. LaMonica followed, holding the gun under his jacket. He faced Lockhart. She removed the key from her shoe and unlocked the trunk. The checks were in plain sight in a large open suitcase with straps. "Drop the briefcase in the trunk and take your checks," LaMonica said. The fat man complied by closing the suitcase and fastening the latches. He jerked the bag out of the trunk and walked backward, wide-eyed, wary, his gun hand inside his coat.

LaMonica and Hartzbecker climbed back into the sedan. LaMonica started the engine. In the rearview mirror, he saw Lockhart turn around. The fat man broke into a clumsy run and fell down. He jumped up quickly and continued on.

"Did you see that!" Sandy said. She broke into hysterical laughter, and her fists alternated pounding her thighs and the dashboard. "The fat bastard fell on his ass!" She roared again.

LaMonica eased the revolver into his belt. He started the engine and drove out of the lot.

"We did it!" Sandy said, clapping her hands like a child. "Twenty-five thousand dollars apiece! I'm out! Out of the shit once and for all!" She stretched out her legs and leaned back in the seat. Her eyes closed. "I'm going to the Canary Islands. I know people there. It's sunny the year round. All the Germans go there for vacation. I'll fit in easily. Maybe I'll get a job in one of the little art galleries. I could stay there for the rest of my life and no one would ask any questions." She ran her hands through her hair. "God, I feel good."

LaMonica steered south onto a freeway leading to the border. He edged into the fast lane. Sandy broke into laughter again over Lockhart's fall. She wiped tears of mirth from her eyes. An overhead sign read "Rest Stop—One Mile."

"I'd better pull over so we can stash the money under the

backseat," LaMonica said. "I'm afraid they might open the trunk when we cross the border. No use taking any chances at this point."

Sandy nodded. She leaned back against the headrest and closed her eyes.

LaMonica swung the sedan onto a side road separated from the freeway by a parking island. The usual California rest stop: a grassy area with cement picnic tables and a restroom facility. It was deserted. He pulled to the end farthest from the entrance and parked. Sandy was still resting, eyes shut.

LaMonica pulled the gun and put it to her temple. Her eyes flew open. "Get out of the car," he said. There was a look of horror on her face. Tears welled in her eyes. She didn't move.

"Open your door and get out. I won't hurt you if you will get out of the car."

"Please don't do this," she said. "All I want is my part. I earned it. I did the things you asked me to do. I don't deserve this. I came across the border for you. I risked everything."

"Get out of the fucking car right now!" LaMonica said.

A tear rolled down her cheek. Still she didn't move. "People told me that you hated women, that you just used them. You're sick." Her hand grasped the door handle. She opened the door and climbed out.

Keeping the pistol trained on her, LaMonica followed her out the passenger side. He pointed toward some trees. "That way . . . move," he said.

Her eyes were wide. "No," she said. "I don't want to go over there. You can have the money. Please don't hurt me." Her hands floated to the surrender position.

LaMonica glanced about. There was the sound of cars zooming by on the freeway, people heading for the border. Stiff-armed, he aimed the weapon at the middle of her back.

He fired.

Sandy flew forward and down, her hands failing to break her fall. LaMonica stepped forward. Aiming at her head, he fired twice. Gasping sounds. Her body twitched about. For a moment he thought he might have heard a sob, but he discounted it as a simple stress reaction. He stepped back. Having looked around again, he pushed the revolver into his back pocket. It was warm.

LaMonica bent at the waist and grasped Sandy's body by the wrists. He dragged it for a long way across the grass to the edge of a small embankment. Without hesitation, he swung the body over the side. Like a mannequin, it rolled along the dirt and grass to the bottom. He stepped back and surveyed the entire area again. He was alone. Before getting back in the car, he hid the revolver in the trunk.

On the way back to Mexico he was careful not to exceed the speed limit.

CHAPTER 23

The restaurant, a twelve-seater, was directly across th
street from the police station. The place was devoid o
decoration except for a set of primitive murals painted o
the rough-textured walls: serape-clad boys riding burros to
ward a setting sun; brown, dark-eyed women toting chi`
dren. There was no air conditioning.

The three cops sat around a Formica table as they waite
to be served. Rodriguez had commanded the Treasur
agents to order the biggest lobster dish. They had followe
orders.

Carr took a sip of Carta Blanca and set the bottle dowr
"Purple ink," he said with a puzzled look.

"I guess we won't find out what LaMonica counterfeite
until something printed with purple ink hits the street,
Kelly said. He stared at one of the wall paintings.

"We may not be that lucky," Carr said. "For all we kno
he counterfeited bank certificates of deposit, or some othe
such security. A scam like that wouldn't be uncovered fc
years."

Everyone nodded.

A chunky, dark-haired woman wearing a peasant dres
strutted out of the kitchen balancing a platter. She set

down on the table. The platter contained a pile of enormous, steaming lobsters. A young girl, who could have been her daughter, followed her with heavy plates brimming with peppers, refried beans, and rice. She made room on the table and set them down.

Kelly smiled graciously. He tucked a paper napkin into his collar. Nothing was said as the three men went about the business of eating. There was only the crunching of shells, sucking noises and the passing of plates.

Suddenly Rodriguez jumped up, knocking his chair backward. *"Tinta morada!"* he cried. Without so much as wiping his hands, he barged out the front door and headed for the police station. Carr and Kelly stopped eating only long enough to shrug.

A few minutes later Rodriguez marched back in the front door holding a single sheet of printed paper with two fingers. He handed the paper to Carr and made a silly bow. He sat down and resumed eating.

Kelly leaned over his partner's shoulder as he read: "Warning Bulletin—Travelers Chex Incorporated, Houston, Texas . . ."

In the middle of the page was a color reproduction of a traveler's check. The basic color of the printing on the check was purple.

"That counterfeit check appeared for the *first time* right here in Ensenada a few days ago," Rodriguez said. He scooped up some beans with the corner of a tortilla and shoveled them into his mouth. "I'll bet that even you gringo *federales* would be able to guess where."

"Teddy's?" Carr said.

Rodriguez chewed for a while and swallowed. "Right. That *pendejo* Teddy Mora deposited the checks in his account at the bank down the street. When they bounced, he told them he had cashed the checks for customers at his bar." Rodriguez laughed sarcastically. "As if he would cash *anything* for the *pendejos* that hang out in that place."

"I'll be damned," Kelly said. He spoke with his mouth full.

"The Travelers Chex security man that came into the

Field Office the other day . . ." Carr said with a furrowe
brow. "This is what he must have been beating around th
bush about. But why the questions about Freddie Roth?"

Kelly pulled a paper napkin out of a dispenser. He wipe
a mustache of drawn butter off his upper lip. "Some stool
probably sold him an old Freddie Roth story." He shook h
head. "Mr. Greenjeans Freddie Roth no less. Snitche
finger him even in death. They should have embalmed hi
with green ink, God rest his soul."

After the meal Carr tried to pay. The chunky lady acte
insulted and said something in Spanish. Rodriguez pinche
her fondly on the cheek. "She said she honors the badge,
he said.

The three returned to the police station. Carr dialed th
telephone number listed on the Travelers Chex circular an
asked for Omar Lockhart. "I'm sorry, sir, but Mr. Lockha
is on business in San Diego," the secretary said. She re
cited a phone number and an address for a motel on Orteg
Road where he could be reached. She asked him to hol
the line. Carr placed his hand over the mouthpiece. "Lock
hart's staying in a motel just up the street from the on
where Luegner's fiasco went down," he said. Kelly wore
puzzled expression.

A man with an authoritative voice came on the line. H
introduced himself as the chairman of the board. Carr tol
him about his visit from Lockhart. He explained about th
search for LaMonica and the discovery of the printin
press.

"What does this fugitive look like?" the chairman asked

"Gray-haired guy with a missing little finger on his le
hand," Carr said.

A brief silence. The chairman moaned. Briefly, he ex
plained what Lockhart was doing in San Diego. "Woul
this counterfeiter you're looking for involve himself i
such a scheme?" he said.

Carr looked at the ceiling. "I'd say that was a definit
possibility."

"I'll have Mr. Lockhart get in touch with you," th
chairman said, a note of urgency in his voice. He hung up

Carr chortled. "It sounds like LaMonica just sold a load of phony traveler's checks to the Travelers Chex company itself. He sold 'em a bill of goods that the package was left over from one of Freddie Roth's old printing runs . . . and they paid him *fifty thousand dollars*."

"Maybe the company preferred to take the loss all at once," Kelly said. "Less paperwork!" The cops broke into hearty laughter. Rodriguez slapped his knee.

As soon as he caught his breath, Kelly said, "Where will LaMonica go now that he's made the big money?"

"Maybe he'll come right back here," Carr said. "He knows the heat is on for him across the line."

"On the other hand, with that much money he could pretty much pick and choose his hideout," Kelly said.

"Good point," Carr said.

Lockhart paid for his room with a traveler's check (all company executives were required to do so on company business—"Avoidance of Possible Adverse Publicity" the memo had been entitled). While checking out, he chatted amiably with the clerk, a mature woman wearing a flowered dress that fluffed over meaty thighs.

The switchboard buzzed. The woman picked up the receiver. "You just caught him," she said. "He's standing right here in front of me." She handed Lockhart the receiver.

It was the chairman.

"I'm glad I caught you before you left," he said angrily. "I just took a call from a U.S. Treasury agent named Carr—"

"Yes sir, I've met him," Lockhart interrupted.

"That's nice," continued the chairman. "He told me some interesting things about a man named LaMonica, a counterfeiter. Seems that this LaMonica may have recently printed up some of our traveler's checks. Carr has evidence that he uncovered down in Ensenada."

"I'll follow up on that immediately, sir," Lockhart said. "Since I'm so close to Mexico, I'll just drive down and gather the pertinent details in person."

"Before you rush off," the chairman said, "you might like to know that this counterfeiter is a gray-haired man with a missing finger on his left hand."

Lockhart felt a rush of heat spread across the back of his neck. The phone felt slippery; he could barely hold it in his hand. He wanted to gag. Nothing was said for a while.

"Are you still there?" the chairman said.

"Yes sir."

"Please don't tell me that you've already bought the checks, Omar. Please don't tell me that," the chairman said. Lockhart pictured him with palm against brow.

"Yes sir. Just a few minutes ago . . . Jesus, sir." Lockhart made a fist. It pressed against his chin.

"You allowed a counterfeiter, a criminal person, to sell us his own product," the chairman said. "You handed over fifty thousand dollars of this year's net profit to someone you hadn't properly checked out. I'm sure I'll have no problem at all explaining that to the other members of the board. Perhaps I can appeal to their goddamn *sense of humor!"*

"I'm sorry . . . sir."

"Fix it, Omar," the chairman said.

"Sir?"

"You're going to go out and repair the damage you've done to us. Do you understand what I'm telling you?"

"Sir . . . uh . . . I'm not exactly sure what I can do at this point," Lockhart said.

"You can go find this LaMonica person and get our money back! That's what you can do! You can go grab this cocksucker by the throat and squeeze until he gives us our money back. Do whatever you have to do. *Nobody is going to do this to us and get away with it."*

"I'll do my best, but I'm not sure I can—"

"Find the dirty sonofabitch and bring back our fifty thousand dollars, Omar. If you don't, your desk won't be here when you return. You made the mess. Now you can clean it up!" The phone clicked loudly. Omar Lockhart handed the receiver to the woman. He rubbed his temples.

His head ached as if acid had been injected behind his eyes.

"Are you all right?" said the woman. She stared at him as if he were bleeding. "Mr. Lockhart? Would you like to sit down?"

Lockhart took out a handkerchief. He wiped his eyes and forehead and took a deep breath. "Mr. Brown's room," he said. "Roger Brown. He checked out a short while ago. That . . . uh . . . was him on the telephone. He asked if I could get a copy of his room's telephone bill. He needed some of the numbers."

The woman opened a drawer and pulled out a stack of receipts. She thumbed through a few and pulled one out of the pile. "He only called one number from his room," she said. The woman wrote the telephone number on a piece of paper and handed it to him.

Lockhart mumbled his thanks. He shuffled out the door.

Having found a pay phone next to the swimming pool, Lockhart dropped in a dime. The operator told him that it was an Ensenada area code. He gave her the number. It rang.

"Teddy's Bar," a man said.

Lockhart slammed the phone down. He headed for his car.

The dirt lot in front of Teddy's Bar was filled with motorcycles: the kind with riser handlebars and chrome decorations of one kind or another. Lockhart parked next to a Harley with a tuck-and-roll leather seat.

The front door of the place was open. There was the sound of raucous conversation, jukebox music, some outright yelling. All in all, it was the kind of place that Omar Lockhart would not have set foot in under any other circumstances. But he was angry. He reached inside his coat and felt the butt of his revolver. I am not going to be afraid of a bunch of motorcycle creeps. I have no argument with them nor they with me, he thought.

Lockhart locked his car, hitched up his trousers, and strode into the front door. The smell of marijuana was overpowering. There was a hush in the conversation as he made his way to the bar. The crowd, a bunch of bearded men and fat women wearing an assortment of leather and denim vests, followed him with their eyes. Two men left their bar stools and strolled out the door.

"Are you the proprietor?" Lockhart said to the skinny man standing behind the bar.

"Proprietor?" the man said sarcastically. "Yes, I am. And who, pray tell, might *you* be? I know you're not the man who comes to drain the cesspool in back. He's already been here and left." The bartender looked to the greasers at the bar, with a punchline smile. They broke into hostile laughter.

Lockhart felt a tingling sensation in his hands as he reached into his wallet for a business card. He handed one of the engraved cards to Teddy Mora. There were eyes on his wallet. He shoved it back into his coat. I'm handling this badly, he thought.

"I'm the director of security for Travelers Chex Incorporated," Lockhart said.

Teddy picked up a flashlight. He flicked it on and held it to the card. "That probably means you're an ex-cop," he said.

"As a matter of fact I was with the police department in Houston for a number of years," Lockhart said.

"Oh, really?" Teddy said. "That's probably some real hot and heavy shit back in good ol' Houston. But down here it doesn't mean *frijoles*. You see, cops ain't welcome in here. This is a foreign country, my man. American cops like you are just run-of-the-mill assholes down here."

A hairy man at the bar belched like a foghorn. People laughed. Lockhart tried to force a smile, but couldn't.

"Is there somewhere where we could speak in private?" Lockhart said. He held his breath.

"No," Teddy said. More laughter.

Lockhart glanced around. Everyone stared. "Some bogus traveler's checks have been passed in here," he said. "The man that is probably responsible uses the name Roger

Brown. He has gray hair and a missing little finger. Do you know him?"

"Yeah, he was here just a little while ago," someone said.

Lockhart turned toward the voice. "Do you know where he went?"

"He went out to take a shit and the bears ate him." An explosion of laughter.

Teddy joined in the merriment. "That's right," he said. "The motherfuckin' *bears* ate him." Suddenly Teddy Mora stopped laughing and leaned across the bar. His face was within an inch of Lockhart's. "Now why don't you get the fuck out of here before we lose our sense of humor."

Lockhart stepped back. He shuffled out the door into the parking lot. His car was gone. There was automobile glass on the ground where he had parked it. He let out a deep breath. "Damn," he said out loud. He rubbed a sleeve across his forehead and headed straight back in the door. He marched directly to the bar. "I want to use your telephone," he said to the bartender. "Someone has stolen my car."

Another burst of laughter. Teddy Mora ignored him. He poured drinks.

"Dammit. Is there a telephone here?" Lockhart said. Suddenly, a hand that smelled like motor oil was over his mouth. His legs flew forward and he was on the floor. Someone was grabbing his gun. Something crashed over his head.

CHAPTER 24

The hospital room was furnished with a pair of beds with hand cranks and a couple of nightstands. The cubicle's solitary window framed nothing more than an alley wall.

Lockhart's eyes were blackened and there was a line of fresh stitches protruding from his upper lip. Both arms were in casts. The Texan spoke slowly, without emotion.

Because of the smell of disinfectant, Carr felt like covering his nose as Lockhart staggered on with his tale. Every few seconds the security man's tongue would dart out to moisten his swollen lips, and then he would continue. Earlier, he had asked for water and Kelly had helped him drink. Rodriguez, leaning against the wall, made notes in what looked like a patrolman's traffic-citation book.

"I regained consciousness on the road near the turnoff to Teddy's Bar," Lockhart said. "A man driving a truck picked me up and brought me here. I passed out again when he pulled me up by my arms." He blinked a few times and took a deep breath. He exhaled. "That's the whole sorry-ass story, I'm afraid. They just plain got the best of me."

"Would you like us to phone your office?" Carr said.

"Thanks anyway," Lockhart said as if in a trance. "That won't be necessary."

"Do you think you'd be able to recognize any of the men who beat you up?" Rodriguez said.

Lockhart licked his lips. "Motorcycle hounds," he said. "All I remember is leather jackets, beards. The whole thing happened so fast . . ." He turned to Rodriguez. "They stole a gun I had with me, as well as my wallet and I.D. I guess that's illegal down here."

"That's okay," said the officer.

A raven-haired nurse entered the room. She poked a pill into Lockhart's mouth and held a glass of water to his lips. The pudgy man drank, then closed his eyes.

The cops left the room and walked through a small office and out the front door. They stood around Rodriguez's squad car for a moment.

"They really worked that poor guy over," Kelly said. "They must've taken turns on him."

Rodriguez beamed as he rubbed his hands together fiendishly. "It's just what I've been waiting for, boys," he said.

"Howzat?" Carr said.

"An excuse to kick Teddy's door in," he said. He swung open the door of the police car and vaulted his lumberjack frame into the driver's seat. Carr and Kelly followed him into the vehicle. Rodriguez started the engine and slammed the car into first gear. He made a U-turn and sped south along the main road. On the way through town, Rodriguez snatched the microphone off the hook on the dashboard and barked commands in Spanish. By the time he had reached the edge of town he was followed by a pair of squad cars loaded with uniformed officers.

Nearing the turnoff to Teddy's Bar, Rodriguez slammed on the brakes. He pulled off the road onto a soft shoulder. The police cars stopped directly behind him. The officers, young men in khaki uniforms who appeared as fit as infantrymen, piled out. They put on their hats and formed an informal line next to Rodriguez's vehicle.

Rodriguez pulled a newspaper from underneath the

driver's seat and stepped out of the car. He spread the paper out on the hood of the car. With rough pen strokes, he drew a diagram of a building. Above it, he wrote "Teddy's." He gave instructions and the officers nodded. Rodriguez said, *"Vamos,"* in a harsh voice. The young officers removed their hats and hustled back to their squad cars.

Rodriguez stepped to the rear of his vehicle and opened the trunk. He pulled out the Thompson submachine gun and checked it. Having done this, he got back in the car and arranged the weapon so that it rested against his thigh, barrel pointed to the floorboard. He started the engine and edged back onto the highway. He pressed the siren button and flicked the switch for the red light. The other squad cars did the same. The raiders raced down the dirt road at full speed, creating an enormous dust cloud. Kelly fastened his seat belt.

"You boys follow me in the front door," Rodriguez said. "Teddy is yours."

Carr nodded.

The police cars skidded to within a few feet of the bar's front door. The parking lot was littered with motorcycles. The officers piled out. Rodriguez, tommy gun at port arms, trotted to the front door. With one mighty kick, he knocked the door fully off its hinges. It fell forward like a gang-plank. He sprang inside. *"Pendejos!"* he said. *"Manos arriba!"* He fired a machine-gun burst into the ceiling. Customers screamed and dived for cover. Plaster fell. The officers rushed in and slammed people against walls. Everyone was frisked.

Carr found Teddy Mora ducking down behind the bar. He reached across and seized the man's collar with both hands. A forceful pull brought him over the bar. Carr dragged the struggling man out the back door. Mora came to his feet swinging. Carr blocked a left and punched Mora squarely in the jaw. The bartender fell to the dirt. As he scrambled to get up, Carr stabbed a knee into his chest. Mora dropped to the dirt again. He gasped for air.

Carr put his hands in his pockets. "Told you I'd be back," he said.

Mora moaned.

"Now I'll ask you again," he said. "Where is Paul La-Monica?"

It was a minute before Mora caught his breath. Hands rubbing his stomach, he sat up. "I don't know," he said.

"Okay," Carr said, "then here's what happens next: the police will camp out in front of this place. They don't like you. They'll be happy to put you out of business, altogether."

"I didn't say I wasn't willing to cooperate," Mora said. "I didn't say that when you talked to me in L.A., and I'm not saying it now. I just don't know where LaMonica *is* right now. I can't tell you something I truly don't know."

"Is he in Mexico?" Carr said.

"I'm not sure," Mora said with a sincere expression. "But he does keep in touch. I'm asking you, do I sound like someone who isn't willing to cooperate? Why should I take heat for LaMonica? He isn't shit to me."

"I'm going back to L.A. tomorrow afternoon," Carr said. "Phone me at the police station before I leave or you're through down here. Rodriguez will run you and all of your asshole biker friends straight across the border. And when you come across, I'll be waiting there for you."

Carr turned and walked back into the bar. Customers were still spread-eagled along the walls. Rodriguez sat at a cocktail table examining a pile of guns and knives. Near the front door, a group of bearded men stood handcuffed to one another. Rodriguez nodded and a policeman ushered the chain of men out the door.

A policeman held open a gunny sack next to the table, and Rodriguez slid the weapons into it. Mora came in the back door. He approached the detective meekly. "Mr. Rodriguez, can I ask what this is all about? I've never had any trouble here before."

Rodriguez pointed to the gunny sack. "You don't call that trouble?" he said. "This is Mexico. We don't like *pen-*

193

dejos who carry guns." He stood up. "Does that tell you *what this is all about,* cocksucker?"

Mora's head was down. Rodriguez stood up and shoved him out of the way. He barked orders in Spanish. The officers headed out the front door. A police van pulled up. The prisoners were loaded into it.

The raiders piled into their squad cars and departed.

"What do you think?" Rodriguez said as he steered onto the highway.

"Hard to predict," Carr said. "What Teddy does will depend on what he's got going with LaMonica right now. He'll probably turn him in if it won't cost him any money."

It was almost closing time for the bars. A camouflage of fog had wafted in from the ocean. Hugging the streets here and there, the cold smoke had turned Ensenada's simple streets into a maze.

Paul LaMonica drove slowly through the motel parking lot. All the rooms were dark and the gold Cadillac wasn't there. He drove out of the lot, turned north and followed the main road, which wound through the deserted shopping district all the way to the bar district at the edge of town. Three people lolled about on the sidewalks in front of barrooms cloistered on a side street blocked off to vehicular traffic. The only light came from a few streetlamps that hung from heavy electrical cord across the thoroughfare. He steered around the corner and into an alley that paralleled the rear entrances to the drinking spots.

Mr. Cool's gold Cadillac was parked in a tiny lot behind the third bar from the corner.

LaMonica pulled into the lot and parked next to the driver's side of the Caddy. After turning off the engine, he rolled down all the windows in his sedan. He removed his windbreaker and folded it into a makeshift pillow. Arranging the jacket on the driver's side, he lay back on the front seat. There was not enough room to stretch out completely, so he positioned his legs at an angle to the passenger door. The only sound in the lot was that of muffled rock tunes coming from inside the bar.

In one motion, LaMonica pulled the .38 from his waist-band and sprang upright in the seat, pointing the gun out of the passenger window. He lay back on the seat. After a while he sprang up again. He tucked the revolver back in his waistband and reclined on the seat to wait. A pair of cats shrieked as they fought up and down the alley. This went on for what seemed like a long time. The noise ceased as a man and woman exited the bar. LaMonica peeked over the seat. Standing just outside the door, they exchanged drunk talk and crotch gropes for a few minutes. The two were young and wore matching cowboy hats with feather bands. The woman giggled as the man pulled down his zipper and urinated against the door of the bar. "Some-one's going to see you. Someone's going to see you," she said in slurred tones. Finally, the man zipped up his fly and they staggered down the alley.

LaMonica lay down on the seat again. He closed his eyes and his mind drifted to the mountain cabin near L.A. He was alone and trapped. His finger was crushed between printing-press rollers. He managed to open a pocket knife. He sawed on the finger and the pain reached up his arm and spread to every part of his body, including his teeth. Finally he saved himself. Blood squirted all over the place.

Paul LaMonica held up the hand with the missing finger and looked at his wristwatch. It was 3:30 A.M. He heard footsteps coming out the back door and heading in his di-rection.

Mr. Cool stood at the driver's door of the Cadillac, fum-bling with car keys.

Using both hands to hold the pistol, LaMonica sprang up in the seat. He held his breath. Aiming the revolver out the window, he fired three shots as fast as he could pull the trigger. With an animal yelp, Mr. Cool slammed forward against the side of the Cadillac and dropped to his knees. LaMonica fired again. As if the fourth shot were charged with electricity, the black man came to his feet and stag-gered toward the alley. LaMonica fired again but missed. He dropped the revolver on the front seat and started the engine. He flew out of the parking space and accelerated into the alley. Mr. Cool had fallen with his back next to the wall on the left. He moaned. LaMonica pulled up next to him and slammed on the brakes. He grabbed the gun off the seat and took aim out the window. Mr. Cool held out a hand. "No more," he said. LaMonica pulled the trigger again and the black man's head exploded. He kicked the pedal to the floor and zoomed down the alley and around the corner.

CHAPTER 25

One by one, the men arrested at Teddy's Bar had refused to talk.

Carr sat with Rodriguez and Kelly around a wooden table in the police station's interview room, waiting for the last prisoner to be sent in. The cubicle, its unfinished plaster walls bearing some indentations with red marks that Carr thought might have been made with a human head, was filled with the odor of fresh oranges. Like a ritual, Rodriguez had peeled and gobbled one orange after each unsuccessful interview.

Rodriguez thumbed his hat off his forehead. He massaged an orange and ripped it in half. Leaning over the wastebasket, he chomped. Juice dripped into the basket. "I told you none of them would tell us anything," he said with his mouth full.

Carr shrugged. Kelly yawned. Rodriguez finished the rest of his orange.

A guard opened the door. He shoved a thirtyish man dressed in greasy Levi's and leather vest into the room. The man had an untrimmed beard and a head of long and knotted hair like a collie's that needed brushing. He was tattooed on both arms, wore an earring, and his hands were chaffed and gray with dirt.

Rodriguez pointed to a chair. The man sat down at the table across from him.

Carr showed the man his badge. "We're U.S. Treasury agents," Carr said. He flipped over a mug shot of Paul LaMonica that was lying on the table. "Do you know this man?"

"I don't know what you're talking about."

"We're not trying to hassle you," Carr said. "The man is a murderer. All I'm asking is that you take a look at the photograph and tell me if you recognize him."

The long-haired man stared Carr in the eye. "I don't see no photograph, pig."

"You might be in a jam because of the guy that you people beat up at Teddy's," Carr said. "You might find yourself doing a little time down here for it. We can help with that if you want to cooperate."

The man glared at Carr, then at Kelly. "Like I said, I don't see no goddamn photograph."

Rodriguez ripped open another juicy orange. "Are you saying that you really can't see the mug shot?" he said angrily. "You actually can't *see* the mug shot even though it's sitting right there in front of you on the table?" He made an exaggerated expression of disbelief.

"You heard what I said, greaseball."

With a catlike motion, Rodriguez reached over the table and grabbed the prisoner's hair. He yanked him fully across the table and locked the man's throat in the crook of his arm. He squeezed and the prisoner gasped for air. With his free hand, Rodriguez mashed the orange pulp into the man's eyes. "Maybe this will help you see, *pendejo!*"

The man made a stifled yelp. Rodriguez squeezed harder. More orange juice ran into the prisoner's eyes. He struggled frantically. Without releasing his grip on the prisoner's neck, Rodriguez stood up and walked to the door with the struggling man. Having opened it, he punched and kicked the blinded man out the door and into the arms of a uniformed officer. He yelled something in Spanish, and the guard dragged the man away.

Rodriguez pulled out a handkerchief. He wiped his hand carefully.

"There's a man who has no appreciation for citrus fruit," Kelly said. They joined in laughter.

A uniformed officer stuck his head in the door and said something in Spanish. Rodriguez turned to the T-men. "Let's go," he said. "They just found the body of an American at the north of town. Teddy Mora's phone number was in his wallet."

Rodriguez steered the radio car off the main street into an alley. The alley was filled with drunken bar patrons who had filtered out to see the action: suntanned Americans wearing shorts and sandals; Mexicans in flowered shirts and *bracero* hats; fat B-girls in red and black cocktail dresses. The crowd made way for the police car. They pulled up to a rope on stanchions that was blocking the alley. Policemen milled about behind it.

Carr and Kelly followed Rodriguez out of the vehicle. Rodriguez yelled orders and policemen extended more rope to block off the other end of the alley.

The body of a black man sat propped against the alley wall. Being careful to avoid stepping on any evidence, Carr moved closer to the body. He knelt down. The neck was tilted grotesquely in death. Carr observed an entrance wound on the left side of the nose. There was blood behind the head on the wall, and the chest was soaked red. He realized it was the FBI informant.

Kelly knelt next to him. "Is that who I think it is?"

"I'm afraid so."

"There will be miles of memos," Kelly whispered. "Miles."

A uniformed policeman holding a Polaroid camera tapped Carr on the arm. He made a "take a picture" gesture. Carr stood up and stepped back. The flashbulb popped.

Carr looked for Rodriguez. The Mexican was standing in front of a police car talking to an officer with sergeant's stripes. He waved at the T-men. Carr and Kelly approached.

"Witnesses," Rodriguez said. A young blond woman wearing a cowboy hat sat in the backseat. A sleeping man used her lap as a pillow. "They're both drunk. They were standing at the end of the alley when they heard shots and saw a car speed by. One of 'em says the car was white, the other green. My officers interviewed people inside the bar. They said the victim stopped in for one beer. He used the pay phone in front of the place. A call that lasted about fifteen minutes. They said he does the same thing almost every night. Sometimes he *takes* calls at the same phone. Strange."

"Probably making his daily report," Carr said. "He was a snitch for the FBI."

"This case gets more interesting all the time," Rodriguez said.

Carr followed the submachine-gun-toting Rodriguez up the motel steps. He heard Kelly trotting through gravel in the driveway to take a position at the rear of the place. Because of the hour, there were no lights on in any of the rooms. At the top of the steps Rodriguez handed Carr the room key he had removed from the dead man's pocket. Standing to the right of the door, he slid the key into the lock. He turned it and the lock snapped open. He pushed the door ajar a few inches and groped for the light switch. He flipped it on. Rodriguez rushed past him into the room, tommy gun first. The room was empty. Having checked the closet and bathroom, Carr strolled to the window and motioned to Kelly. Kelly holstered his revolver and headed toward the steps.

Rodriguez laid his submachine gun on the bed and proceeded to upturn the nightstand drawers.

Carr rummaged through a suitcase lying open on the dresser table. It was filled with men's clothing. He slammed it shut and pulled open the dresser drawers. Among socks and bathing suits he found form letters from a federal parole officer, credit-card receipts, book matches from L.A. bars he knew as crook hangouts, roach holders, a cutting mirror, a silver cocaine spoon, two driver's licenses in different names bearing the dead man's photograph, and a snub-nosed .38 revolver.

Rodriguez came out of the closet with a woman's straw purse. He emptied it onto the dressing table in front of Carr. Among tubes of lipstick, wadded Kleenex, and bottles of nail polish was a wallet. Rodriguez picked it up and pulled out a gasoline credit card. "Sandra Hartzbecker," he said. He handed the card to Carr.

Carr stared at the credit card for a moment. "She used to pass counterfeit money for LaMonica," he said.

"Small world," Kelly said on his way in the door. He strode to the bed, grasped the mattress with both hands and flipped it onto the floor. A notebook was lying on top of the box spring. He picked it up and quickly thumbed through the pages. "Dope notations," he said matter-of-factly. He tossed the book on the floor.

The telephone on the nightstand rang.

Rodriguez picked up the receiver. He nodded a few times, then made exclamations in Spanish. He yanked his pen and notepad out of his pocket and sat down on the bed. After completing some brief notes, he gave instructions and then hung up. "A teletype just came in from the San Diego Police Department," he said. "They found the body of Sandra Hartzbecker. She was shot and dumped alongside a freeway. They found a motel key to this room on her and requested that we search it for clues."

"I'll be damned," Kelly said. His thumbs were planted in his belt.

Carr stepped to the window. The view was of a cluster of wooden shanties webbed with clotheslines that were partially hidden behind the only modern building in town. Carr knew it was a sports betting office. A dry riverbed spotted with gardens of algae ran in front of the inhabited area. It was littered with empty milk cartons and other detritus. He stared blankly at the scene for a moment, then returned to the dresser. Taped to the corner of the mirror was a swimsuit photograph of Mr. Cool and Sandra Hartzbecker frolicking on the beach. The black man was in a weight-lifter's pose. Sandra Hartzbecker stood next to him, feigning amazement as she tested one of his puffed biceps. Carr pulled the photograph from the mirror and stared at it for a moment. He tossed it in the wastebasket.

"LaMonica is covering his tracks," Carr said.

"Permanently," Kelly said.

Paul LaMonica, briefcase in hand, knocked loudly on the door of Teddy's Bar for the third time. He looked at his wristwatch. It was almost 10:00 A.M.

Finally, Teddy Mora opened the peephole. "We've got a lot to talk about," Mora said. He closed the peephole. The sound of a dead bolt snapping open. Mora swung open the door.

LaMonica stepped inside and gave a quick glance around. The bar smelled like a mixture of stale beer and marijuana. It was dark except for a shaft of gray light emanating from a window in the corner.

Teddy Mora closed the door and locked it. He was clad only in a pair of too-big boxer shorts.

LaMonica sauntered behind the bar. Having set the briefcase down, he poured a shot of tequila. "Where's the lemon?" he said.

Mora shuffled to the bar. He pointed to a plastic container. "The goddamn feds rousted the shit out of me at that motel. I've been trying to get in touch with you. They jumped on me like hobos on a hot dog, ripped my camper truck apart. I deserve a fuckin' explanation—"

"That's over now," LaMonica interrupted. He lifted the shot glass and swigged his tequila. "You were clean. You had nothing to worry about. The snitch was Sandy's dude boyfriend."

"That filthy—"

"He's dead," LaMonica interrupted again. He chomped on a lemon slice.

Teddy Mora's jaw dropped open. "No lie?" he said.

"No lie."

"Teddy's not even going to ask Paulie the Printer how it went down," Mora said. An exaggerated wink.

LaMonica poured another shot of tequila, picked up a knife, and sliced off another piece of lemon.

"Some feds and the local pigs were here looking for you," Mora said as he crawled onto a bar stool. "They shot holes in the roof and slapped a few of the bikers around. It was because of a traveler's-check guy that came in looking for you. We kicked his ass till his *nose* bled." Mora smiled. "This was a favor from Teddy to Paulie the Printer."

La Monica drank the tequila and bit into a lemon slice. "How are things with the Barber?"

Mora stared at him for a moment. His eyes lit up. "I just spoke to him yesterday. He's ready to deal."

"I've got my part of the money," LaMonica said.

Mora gulped. "All of it?" he said.

Paul LaMonica unlocked the latches on the briefcase and flipped it open. "All of it," he said.

Mora's mouth dropped open, then stretched into a broad grin. He reached across the bar and slapped the other man on the shoulder. "I knew you'd do it," he said. "There was never one single fucking moment that Teddy doubted you'd be able to come up with the money. With anyone else I would have had some doubts about whether they could produce, but not Paulie the Printer. He's a man of his word. I've always said that and I'll fucking say it again."

LaMonica turned his head to avoid Mora's morning-after breath. "So let's do the deal," he said. "The sooner the better."

Teddy Mora swept fingers through his sticky hair. "I know where you're coming from; cops nosing around here after you. You're thinking why not get the thing *over with?* I'm with you one hundred and fifty percent."

"Can we do it today?" LaMonica said.

Mora slapped LaMonica's shoulder again. "There's no reason why not." He ambled behind the bar and grabbed the telephone. He dialed. Words in Spanish . . . *"Bueno, bueno,"* he said and hung up the receiver. "I've set up a meeting with my local snowman. I'll see what he says. If we can do the deal today, so much the better."

"I'll come along," LaMonica said, "since I'm laying half the action."

Mora shook his head. "We both know that you have the right to negotiate—but I know my man. He'll shy away from doing any quick deal once he meets a new face. You know how dealers are. He'll want to have a drink and get used to you before he'll talk business. But he *knows* me. I can give him any number of bullshit reasons why I need to do a rapid-fire deal. Coming from me, he'll go for it. The man trusts me. We go way back. What I'm saying is if you want to come along, I'm all for it, but it will complicate what could be an easy wham-bam-thank-you-ma'am coke deal."

LaMonica's hands were perspiring. Deliberately he wiped them on his trousers. "I take it that you are ready to stand behind the deal. You're vouching for the connection? You're telling me that your man has cocaine and not powdered sugar?"

Mora folded his broomstick arms across his chest. He looked LaMonica in the eye. "I am," he said.

LaMonica's smile was sardonic. "To me that means if the thing goes sour, you are accepting total responsibility."

"I guess you could look at it like that," Mora said. "I'm putting up fifty grand just like you are, but I'm not worried. Sitting here looking you right in the eye, I can truthfully and honestly tell you that I am not in the least bit fucking worried." He wiped an ash off the bar and folded his arms again.

LaMonica's hands touched the tequila bottle. "Just *so* there are no misunderstandings . . ." he said. "What I am saying is that if anything *does* go wrong, I personally will send you to the funeral parlor."

Mora spoke without hesitation. "Like I said, I'm not worried." He looked at his wristwatch. His Adam's apple bobbed up and down for a moment before he spoke. "While I'm meeting the man and putting things together, you'd better stay right here. Stay inside and don't go out.

The cops have already been here. They will figure I've tipped you and told you to stay away from the joint. They would never think to come back."

Teddy Mora dressed quickly in the liquor storeroom where LaMonica knew he slept on a cot. Mora walked back out into the bar area with a glass bottle of cologne shaped like a boot. He dabbed it on his neck immoderately. "Leave it to Teddy," he said on his way out the door.

Paul LaMonica drank another tequila. He felt an alcohol twinge in his stomach. He wished he had eaten breakfast.

CHAPTER 26

The Ensenada police station was quiet. Rodriguez mumbled into the telephone. Carr sat next to Rodriguez's desk. Fatigued, he tapped a pencil on his knee and stared at a calendar on the wall in front of him. He bit his lip as he remembered that he was supposed to have taken Sally to dinner the night before. She'd told him she had tickets to a play . . . or was it a jazz recital? Should he call her and apologize?

Kelly sat at a small desk in the corner. He sorted through the items taken from Sandra Hartzbecker's hotel room. "Now what the hell do we do?" he said without looking up.

Rodriguez set the receiver down. He rolled his chair against the wall behind him. He stretched, and loosened his necktie. "My men have checked every motel in town. Every one of my informants has been shown LaMonica's mug shot. No bites. Which in this small town means that someone is either hiding LaMonica or he's gone back across the border. If he can make his own phony I.D., he can slide across any time he wants."

"I figure him for being down here," Carr said. "But I'm not sure what else we can do to find him. Teddy Mora is

LaMonica's only connection that we know of. We've hit him and it didn't do any good."

"We can hit him again," Rodriguez said, "but Teddy knows I don't have the pull to put him out of business. A Mexican businessman here in town fronted for his bar license because it's illegal for Americans to own property down here. Teddy is insulated."

The telephone on Rodriguez's desk rang. He answered it. "Hold the line," he said. He handed the receiver to Carr.

"Is this Agent Carr?" Mora's tone was impassive. "Teddy Mora here. I need to talk with you alone."

"What do you want to talk about?" Carr said.

"Paul LaMonica."

"I'm listening."

"I don't like to talk on the telephone. Can we meet somewhere?"

"You name it."

"How about the abandoned campgrounds at the south end of town."

"I like public places," Carr said.

"I understand," Mora replied. "How about the International Sports Book Office. Say in half an hour?"

"See you there." Carr set the receiver down and lit a cigarette. "Teddy wants to meet," he said.

Charles Carr parked his sedan in a small parking lot situated between the riverbed and a prefabricated building the size of a gymnasium. He locked the car and headed in the front door. Inside, the structure looked like a warehouse except for a wall of betting windows with signs in both English and Spanish. Racing forms and newspapers littered the cement floor. Above the cashier's windows a man on an elevated walkway scratched Caliente race results on a green chalkboard extending the entire width of the building. Preoccupied Mexican and American men, only a few of whom were in groups, sat at the tables that covered the expanse of the floor. There was little discussion in the place.

Teddy Mora, dressed in a tan bush jacket and wearing

wraparound sunglasses, sat alone at a table. Carr approached him and sat down. He smelled cologne.

"Do you bet the ponies?" Mora said without looking up from a racing form he was studying.

"Sometimes," Carr said. "When I get a tip."

Mora dug a pen out of a flap pocket and circled the name of a horse. "I like your style, Carr. You remind Teddy of the old days in L.A. The rounders in town knew that if you fucked with the feds you were likely to end up taking the bus to Terminal Island. The feds would do anything to sink you. Years ago I saw a couple of you fellas kick the crap out of one of Mickey Cohen's bodyguards in broad daylight right in front of a bar on Sunset Boulevard. After they worked him over, they arrested him for assault on a federal officer. The way you people came right across the border looking for LaMonica reminded me of the old days. I know it's against your rules for you people to come down here, but you did it anyway. *Just like the good old days*, I said to myself."

"Where is Paul LaMonica?" Carr said.

"When Teddy called he didn't say he was going to turn him in," Mora said. "He just invited you to come down and talk."

"Here I am," Carr said.

Mora filled some numbers in on a betting slip. He shoved the slip into his pocket. "I didn't call you down here to waste your time. I can offer you LaMonica on a silver platter if things can be worked out to my satisfaction."

"What will *satisfy* you?" Carr said sarcastically.

"Three things. I want a ten-thousand-dollar reward for telling you where to find LaMonica. I want my possession case in L.A. dismissed. I want the heat taken off my bar and my customers that were arrested, released. Without your promise on all three items, I can tell you right now that you will *never* find Paul LaMonica. I guess you know he has access to all the phony identification he wants. I guess you know that."

"Where can you deliver him?" Carr said.

"Right here in Ensenada."

"I want him in the U.S.," Carr said.

Mora removed his sunglasses. There were red marks on the bridge of his nose. He massaged them and replaced the glasses. "I might be able to work something out along those lines if everything else sounds right. And you'll dismiss my counterfeit case?"

"The U.S. attorney should go along with that in exchange for LaMonica."

"And the ten-grand reward?"

"Ten grand is out of the question," Carr said. "But I can probably get you a grand. Money's been tight this year."

"I need ten grand to pay my lawyer on the possession case."

"No you don't," Carr said. "You told the U.S. magistrate you were unemployed and he appointed the public defender for you."

Teddy Mora rubbed the bridge of his nose again. "You really do remind me of the old days, Carr."

"Then we have a deal?"

"Snitching off LaMonica is not worth the risk unless you can guarantee that Rodriguez will take the heat off my bar."

"I can ask him," Carr said. "He'll probably go along with the program."

"Can you guarantee that?"

"I can't guarantee anything."

"I'm not sure it's worth the risk. I'll think about it and let you know."

Carr stood up and left.

Paul LaMonica lay on the storeroom cot where he had been since Teddy left, his feet resting on the black briefcase. His eyes were closed, and he could hear the murmur of the ocean. The hunger he had felt had gone away, as had the ringing in his ears he'd suffered from firing out of the car. The cot was firm and he was not uncomfortable.

A key slipped into the front-door lock.

LaMonica vaulted from the cot. He grabbed the briefcase and drew his revolver, aiming it at the door as he approached cautiously.

"It's me," Teddy Mora said. "Everything is okay." Mora entered the room carefully, hands over his head. LaMonica stepped outside the door and looked around for a moment. He returned inside and stuffed the revolver back in his belt.

Teddy Mora grabbed some bar napkins off a table and wiped his brow. "Relax," he said. "Teddy has this thing almost put together." He looked at the napkins and wadded them in his hand. "The man agreed to do a quick deal as a personal favor to me." He turned and headed toward the bar. Having poured a shot glass of tequila and tossed it back, he coughed a string of saliva. "Went down the wrong pipe," Mora muttered as he pounded his chest. Taking a few deep breaths, he made his way to a cocktail table and sat down. He waved LaMonica to a chair.

LaMonica ignored the gesture. "Let's hear it," he said.

"Now all we do is head for the bank where I have my money on deposit. The manager is wired. He'll be expecting us. You make your deposit and then we wait at a pay phone for a call. The dope will be stashed in a car parked in the pay lot on the American side of the border. *We won't even have to sweat getting the load across.* One of their mules will have already taken care of that for us. It's *their* risk, not ours. This is the goddamn *beauty* of it. We take delivery on the U.S. side. We drive over, pick it up, and head for Hollywood. The Barber will be waiting. By ten o'clock tonight we'll be counting our shekels. The deal will be done."

"Do you mean to tell **me** you've agreed to *front* the money on this side of the border?" LaMonica said. "I don't like it. What if they just take our hundred grand and say thanks?"

"You know as well as I do that all deals down here involve front money," Mora said. "These Mexicans won't deal any other way."

"I don't like it," LaMonica said. He realized he was holding his briefcase and felt foolish. He tossed it on a chair.

"I'm already committed to the deal," Mora said. "My fifty G's are going up front. If you want to back out, I'll try to get credit somewhere for the other fifty. But give me an answer right away, because I'm going to have to reach out quickly for the rest of the buy money. I'm committed to the deal and it's got to go."

LaMonica stared at the briefcase for a moment. He looked Mora in the eye. "And you are personally standing behind the deal?"

Mora stood up. He unzipped his trousers and adjusted his shorts. "Yes, I am. I am that confident."

Teddy Mora parked his camper truck in front of the bank, a brown brick building with a bay window.

LaMonica looked around carefully. He climbed out of the vehicle and waited for Mora to lock the car doors. Next door to the bank was a bluish neon sign balanced over a curtained entrance. The word *Rene's* flashed on and off. And on either side of the door were black-and-white photographs of women wearing sequined G-strings and pasties.

Though it was at least ninety degrees, LaMonica felt cold, as if a block of ice had been fastened to the small of his back. Icy headache. Frozen vertebrae. In prison he had lost full nights of sleep because of that sensation. He touched the butt of the revolver in his waistband. He followed Mora into the bank.

Mora spoke briefly in Spanish with a well-dressed young man sitting at a desk. Mora pointed to LaMonica's briefcase. More businesslike discussion. Mora nodded. LaMonica handed over the briefcase. The manager took it behind a teller's cage. After a while, he returned carrying a receipt and the emptied briefcase. He handed both items to Mora. The two shook hands and exchanged more words in Spanish. LaMonica followed Mora out of the bank. Mora handed the receipt to LaMonica. On it was written "TRS-714." LaMonica questioned the notation.

"That's the license number of the car that the coke will be stashed in," Mora said. "He told me the car is a green Chevy and will be parked in the northwest corner of the border parking lot. Now all we do is have a drink and wait for final delivery instructions."

LaMonica looked at his wristwatch. The cold feeling had not gone away. Teddy Mora led the way into Rene's, a dark place with a runway protruding from a tiny stage. Two old, overweight women wearing frayed chiffon cocktail dresses sat at the bar.

Mora shuffled to the end of the bar and took a seat near a pay telephone. LaMonica followed and sat down next to him. The bartender, a bloated man with thick, ebony hair that looked wet, set bar napkins in front of them. They ordered drinks. Mora pointed a thumb at the wall phone. "Our call will be coming in on that phone," he said. "If they say 'George is home,' we head for the border. That's the okay signal. If they say anything else it means that the deal has been queered. We walk back into the bank and pick up our money. This is the beauty of the deal. The bank man looks out for everybody's interest. He's part of their operation, but he's a legit businessman. He's not going to do anything to piss anyone off and then sit there every day at his desk waiting for somebody to throw a bomb through his front window. Right?"

"If you say so."

The bartender served drinks. Teddy Mora tossed the man a five-dollar bill and told him to keep the change. He sipped, and wiped his mouth with the back of his hand. "Damn! I forgot to call one of the boys to have them open up the bar while you and I are in Hollywood." He stood up and lifted the phone receiver off the wall hook. He dropped in a peso and dialed. Shaking his head, he hung up and removed the peso. "I'd better use another phone," he said. "If they call in and this one is busy it could screw things up." Mora headed for the door. "Be back in a sec," he said as he flapped through the curtain door.

Paul LaMonica picked up his drink and walked slowly to the door. He peeked out the curtain. Teddy Mora stood at a sidewalk pay phone across the street fumbling for change.

CHAPTER 27

The phone rang. Rodriguez picked up the receiver. "Policia de Ensenada," he said. "Yes, he's here. Hold the line." He made a thumbs-up gesture and handed the phone to Carr. Kelly deftly picked up an extension line and cupped his hand over the speaker.

"LaMonica is going to be in the border parking lot, on the U.S. side, at about four P.M. today," Mora said, speaking in low tones. "You should look for a green Chevrolet with California license plate TRS-714. That's T-R-S-7-1-4. It'll be parked in the northwest corner of the lot. You may see me with him. When you arrest him, all I ask is that you make it look like I escaped; you could have someone act like he's chasing me. I'll run back across the border into Mexico. This is to protect my identity as the informer. I mean, like you owe me at least that much for setting him up for you. Agreed?

"One more thing," Mora said. "After you arrest him, I'd appreciate it if you could drop a story on him about how you found a load of cocaine in the trunk of the green Chevy; like a couple of hundred grand's worth. You could tell him you turned it over to the federal narcs or some such shit. The story would help to keep me cool."

"I'll take care of it," Carr said.

"Any questions?" Mora said.

"Is he carrying?"

"A .38 in his belt usually," Mora said. He coughed. "He lets his shirt hang out."

"When you hear me holler 'Freeze,'" Carr said, "get away from LaMonica fast. If you are in a car, jump out. If you are standing near him, run like hell."

"Got it," Mora said. "Say, tell me the truth, did you think I'd really call up and hand over Paulie the Printer?"

"Not really," Carr said, looking at Kelly. "It's a real nice surprise."

Kelly jabbed an extended middle finger at the mouthpiece of the receiver in his hand.

After a few minutes, Mora returned to his seat at the bar. The two men sat awhile in silence. The B-girls whispered to one another and climbed off their bar stools. As they approached the end of the bar, Mora waved them back rudely. "We're not interested," he said.

The bartender frowned at Mora. Mora threw up his hands. "Go ahead," he said. "Buy 'em a drink on me. Business is business, right, *amigo?*" He pulled money out of his pocket and tossed it on the bar. The bartender smiled and poured drinks for the women.

During the next hour Mora made lively talk about other big scores, movie stars who he knew bought jewelry and furs from burglars, and his plans for buying a Hollywood discoteque. LaMonica half listened.

Finally the telephone rang.

As Mora spun his bar stool, Paul LaMonica grabbed his arm, "I'll take it," he said. Mora stared at him as if he wanted to protest, but said nothing.

LaMonica stood and picked up the receiver.

"George is home," the bank manager said. The phone clicked. LaMonica repeated the phrase.

Teddy Mora jumped off his bar stool. He clapped his

hands together. "I told you everything would be a *go*. A one-hundred-percent *go*. We're heading for Hollywood."

LaMonica followed him out the front door.

Kelly steered into the parking lot and cruised slowly. American tourists milled in and out of the enormous lot toting border-town souvenirs: cheap pottery, straw baskets, stuffed iguanas. At one end of the lot was a gate leading to a pedestrian walkway across the international boundary into Tijuana.

The green Chevrolet was parked at the end of a row of vehicles next to a high fence that spanned the perimeter of the parking lot. "There it is," Carr said.

Kelly wheeled the G-car into an open stall a few rows behind the Chevrolet. He turned off the engine. "How do you think we should work it?"

Carr rubbed his chin for a moment. "I say we let him get right up to the Chevy. That'll put him in the corner of the lot with nowhere else to go. You take the right, I'll take the left. Teddy will be able to run either way." He looked at his watch.

Kelly pulled out his revolver and spun the cylinder. He snapped it closed. "I'd feel a lot better if there weren't so many people in and out of this parking lot."

"Me too," Carr said.

Nothing much had been said during the brief trip from Ensenada to Tijuana. Teddy Mora pulled up to a stop light on the outskirts of town.

"You're quiet," he said, glancing at LaMonica. "I get the same way when I'm right in the middle of something. It's probably just concentration."

The light changed. Mora turned onto a road which paralleled the high chain-link fence that marked the U.S. border. Steering with his forearms for a moment, he lit a cigarette and puffed. "A suggestion," he said. "I could let you out a block or so away from the border crossing. You could walk straight across into the parking lot and pick up the load. I could meet you up the street across from the tourist information center. That way we could avoid driving through the crossing point, making a U-turn, and driving back into the lot. You have to admit, if some border pig just happened to notice that kind of an act he might get a little suspicious."

LaMonica leaned back in the seat. "Good idea," he said. "But why don't *you* walk over and pick up the package? I'd rather drive."

Teddy Mora sucked deeply on his cigarette. He spoke with a mouthful of smoke. "Uh, this car isn't registered to you. It might cause a problem at the crossing point."

"Maybe you're right." LaMonica rolled his window down to clear out some of Mora's smoke. "We'll both walk to the lot to make the pickup."

Mora fidgeted. "Is there anything wrong? You haven't said shit since we left Ensenada. I mean if you think there's a better way to do this, just say the word."

LaMonica turned to the other man. His expression was blank. "As long as things go right, there's nothing to talk about."

They passed through the border checkpoint with no problem. Mora drove less than a mile north, pulled over into the middle lane, and made a U-turn. They headed back toward the border.

LaMonica grabbed the steering wheel and tugged. The vehicle veered to the right shoulder of the road. Mora slammed on the brakes. "I'll drive," LaMonica said. He got out of the car and walked around to the driver's side. They exchanged seats. LaMonica put the car in gear and headed toward the parking lot. He stopped a few feet away from the entrance and got out of the car. At the fence he grasped the chain link and stared into the lot for what seemed like a long time. He climbed back in the driver's seat and put the car in gear.

Mora was pale. "It pays to be careful," he said. "Paulie the Printer takes things one step at a time."

LaMonica steered into the parking lot. Though he noticed the green Chevrolet almost immediately, he drove by it, continuing among the rows of vehicles.

Mora pointed. "That was it. You just passed it," he said.

Carr and Kelly ducked below window level of the sedan. They almost bumped heads. "That sneaky sonofabitch is casing the lot," Kelly whispered.

Carr peeked above the dashboard. He pulled his revolver out of its shoulder holster. "He's turning around . . . heading toward the Chevy. This is it."

Kelly's gun was out.

LaMonica pulled up behind the green Chevrolet. A young woman was loading straw baskets into the trunk of a sports car parked next to the vehicle. He slid the revolver out of his waistband. "Get out and get the package," he said.

Mora stared at the weapon. "Everything is cool," he muttered on his way out the door. He ambled to the rear of the vehicle. Keeping his eyes on LaMonica, he reached into the right rear wheel well and fished around.

LaMonica climbed out of the car, holding the gun under his shirt. "Is it there?" he said.

Mora pulled out a key and held it up. He winked.

Charles Carr kept low, moving between automobiles. Kelly flanked on his right two cars away. Finally, only one car separated him from the Chevrolet. Holding his revolver with both hands, Carr sprung from behind it. He aimed at LaMonica. "Freeze! Federal officers!" he said. Mora ran.

With what seemed like an almost practiced motion, LaMonica grabbed the young woman standing at the sports car by her hair. She screamed as he pulled her in front of him. He pressed a pistol to her temple.

Mora darted between cars. LaMonica swung the revolver in his direction and fired once. Mora dropped. He bellowed in pain.

LaMonica pulled the screaming woman closer to him.

Carr drew a bead on LaMonica's forehead. Carefully he

pulled back on the trigger. The woman's head bobbed in the way. He released tension.

"I'll kill her!" LaMonica shouted. "Get back or I'll splatter her brains all over this lot!" Using the woman as a shield, he backed toward his car.

Carr ducked down. He motioned to Kelly. The Irishman vaulted across the hood of a car and grabbed LaMonica's gun hand. They struggled with the weapon. The woman fell down. The gun fired in the air.

Carr aimed. He pulled the trigger.

Paul LaMonica's head snapped backward violently. A spray of blood stained the hood of the car. Kelly grabbed the woman and pulled her away as LaMonica slumped to the ground. She screamed gibberish and thrashed about hysterically. Kelly grabbed her arms and pulled her away. People yelled and ran about frantically. Carr took a few steps forward. He picked up LaMonica's gun and stuck it in his belt. He bent down. His fingers touched the wounded man's neck. There was no carotid pulse.

Carr found Teddy Mora on the pavement lying between two cars. He was doubled up in a ball, his features ashen, lips blue. He was bleeding.

A police car with red lights flashing zoomed into the parking lot and sped up to Carr. The T-man held his badge over his head. "Ambulance!" he said. The officer grabbed the microphone off the dashboard.

By the time the ambulance arrived, Mora had stopped breathing. The ambulance attendant complained to Carr about having been called out on a dry run. With an angry squeal of brakes, he departed.

CHAPTER 28

For Carr and Kelly, the rest of the day was taken up with interviews conducted by the San Diego sheriff's detectives, signing statements and forms and making telephone calls.

It was midnight by the time the agents arrived back in Los Angeles. At Kelly's insistence, Carr steered off the freeway at Vermont and headed for Calhoun's hot-dog stand. He parked in a no-parking zone in front of the place.

Calhoun loaded the counter in front of them with hot dogs and steaming cups of coffee. Kelly unwrapped a frankfurter and, holding it with three fingers, inserted fully half of it into his mouth. He chomped and tore the hot dog in half.

"What do you hear from your son?" Carr asked Calhoun.

"Tyrone called me from basic training this morning. The drill sergeant picked him as a squad leader. He sounded like he was real proud of himself."

"They always pick the tallest guys," Kelly said with his mouth full.

"I can't wait for the basic training graduation," Calhoun said. "I'm going to drive up to Fort Ord to see it. My boy will be marching and standing tall, and I'll be right there in the stands watching." He slapped together a second round of hot dogs and set them on the counter. Neither man made the usual protestations.

"You both look like you could use some sleep," Calhoun said.

The next morning Carr sat at his desk and turned the pages of the operations manual marked "Shooting Policy." There was an atmosphere of military decorum in the office —a remarkable quiet; none of the usual horseplay or swearing. Most of the special agents had found something to do in the field. The secretaries and clerks were dutifully at their desks rather than gossiping in the coffee room. Someone had covered the counterfeiting squad room's Supreme Court photograph (monkeys in dresses sitting around a table) with a map.

It was the usual atmosphere that prevailed in the office whenever the inspectors came to town.

Carr turned a page. He read:

In the event a Special Agent has reason to believe he is in fear of his life, or the lives of others, he is authorized to fire his issued Treasury revolver (Ref. Manual Sect. 387.90) for the purpose of stopping the suspect from committing whatever act he may be engaged in, keeping paramount in his mind the safety of others . . .

Kelly sauntered into the squad room. He took off his suit jacket and tossed it on a rack.

Carr looked at his wristwatch. "My, my," he said, "two full hours."

"I figured while I was in there, I might as well come clean. I copped out on every time we'd violated the manual regulations," Kelly said with a wry smile.

"If you'd done that it would have taken you a lot longer than two hours." Carr flipped the manual shut.

Kelly peeked out into the hallway. "It's Heckel and

Jeckel. They tried to get me to say that there was some other alternative other than shooting . . . the usual second-guessing bullshit. No Waves chimes in with meaningless questions every few minutes. God, I hate that asshole."

"Heckel and Jeckel?" Carr said.

"The two jerks that were out here the time Howard Dumbrowski beat up his next-door neighbor."

Carr nodded.

Special Agent in Charge Norbert T. Waeves, pipe jutting from jaw, slipped into the room. He made his usual entrance, sort of a quick slide around the doorjamb hoping to catch a few words of conversation. He puffed smoke and took the pipe out of his mouth, said, "We're ready for you now, Carr," and made an about-face. He marched back to his office.

Carr followed. Heckel and Jeckel sat on a sofa on either side of a tape recorder. Both men appeared to be in their middle thirties, wore dark suits with striped neckties, and were overweight. Strangely, they looked almost like brothers. Neither acknowledged his presence.

Waeves scooted behind his oversized desk. He pointed Carr to a chair. "I guess you know who these gentlemen are?" he said.

Carr stared at the pair. The tape recorder wasn't running. "Jehovah's witnesses?" he asked.

The trio of inquisitors exchanged somber glances. Heckel turned on the recorder. Jeckel said, "Interview with Special Agent Charles Carr, tape number two, Shooting Incident Analysis." He cleared his throat. "Agent Carr, the operations manual section 302.2 requires that you answer each and every question put to you by an inspector fully and completely. Failure to do so would subject you to administrative action which could result in loss of pay or termination from government service. We take it you are familiar with that section?" He looked at his notes.

Carr nodded.

"Respond verbally, please," Jeckel said.

"Yes," Carr said.

Heckel looked at Jeckel. He nodded. Jeckel looked at his notes for a moment. "When you fired your service revolver," he said, "what was the thought that was foremost in your mind? I mean, right *at* that very moment."

Carr made a thoughtful expression. He leaned forward in his chair. His elbows rested on his thighs. He rubbed his chin for a while. "Things happened fast," he said finally, "but I remember clearly what was going through my mind." A chin rub.

The inspectors made notes.

"I was sort of talking to myself," he continued. "I said, 'Carr, right now you have reason to fear for your life and the lives of others. You are now authorized to fire your Treasury revolver for the purpose of stopping the suspect from committing the act he is engaged in.'" He sat up straight.

Both men frowned. They looked at one another.

"Why did you fire at the suspect's head?" Heckel said.

"It was the only portion of his body that was exposed," Carr said. "The hostage was in front of him."

"Did you consider that you might have missed LaMonica and hit the hostage?" Jeckel threw the question out like a challenge.

"No," Carr said.

"In other words, that possibility didn't even enter your mind. Is that what you're saying?" Heckel said.

"Yes."

"Why not?" Jeckel said.

"Because I've qualified 'expert' at the pistol range every month for over twenty years," Carr said without inflection.

Waeves emitted a burst of pipe smoke. The inspectors wrote things in the margins of their notes. There was a long silence before the next question.

Carr returned to the squad room after the interview. He plopped down at his desk.

Kelly was having an animated telephone conversation. "Thanks a lot for calling," he said. He hung up the receiver. "That was Rodriguez," he said. "He says Teddy Mora's ex–brother-in-law just put a fifty-grand down payment on a motel in Ensenada. He's the manager of the local bank."

"At least somebody came out all right on the deal," Carr said. He gave a little laugh.

Charles Carr strolled with Sally along the cement walkway running parallel to the snack shops and apartment houses that faced Santa Monica Beach. It was the first time they had been together since Carr's return from Mexico. They were lost in a parade of roller skaters and joggers of both sexes, all cocoa-tanned and costumed in skimpy swim clothes. A lithe couple on wheels a few feet in front of them did a ritual of figure eights around one another as they gabbled about the best way to mix margaritas.

Sally had been walking with her head down most of the way. Carr felt like telling her to get whatever it was off her chest, but didn't.

The roller skaters finished their discussion and zoomed away holding hands.

"Why didn't you mention to me that you were going to Mexico?" Sally said. "We were together just hours before you left and you didn't so much as mention it."

"I guess I just didn't think of it," Carr said.

"Did you have a good time?"

Carr didn't answer.

"You don't have to answer that," she said condescendingly. "Rose Kelly said you and Jack had a fabulous lobster dinner down there."

"It was real nice."

Sally stopped in her tracks. She locked her arms across her chest. "There is no reason in the world why you can't share little things like that with me," she said angrily. "We just don't *share* things like other . . . uh . . . friends do. And I think I know why. You're afraid of things becoming too serious. You think that I'm going to put restraints on you. Well, there needn't be chains and boundaries on our relationship. I've proved that. So please stop treating me like some dizzy schoolgirl."

Carr put his arm around her shoulder. He pulled her close to him. They walked on for a while without speaking.

"I would appreciate seeing you more than once or twice a month," Sally said.

"Sounds good," Carr said.